GRAPHIC NOVEL

Francisco Jiménez
Adapted by **Andrew J. Rostan**
Illustrated by **Celia Jacobs**

CLARION BOOKS
IMPRINTS OF HARPERCOLLINSPUBLISHERS

CLARION BOOKS IS AN IMPRINT OF HARPERCOLLINS PUBLISHERS.
HARPERALLEY IS AN IMPRINT OF HARPERCOLLINS PUBLISHERS.

THE CIRCUIT GRAPHIC NOVEL

LIBRARY OF CONGRESS CONTROL NUMBER: 2023932484
ISBN 978-0-35-834821-4 — ISBN 978-0-35-834822-1 (PBK.)

THE ARTIST USED PEN AND INK ON WATERCOLOR PAPER WITH DIGITAL COLOR TO CREATE THE ILLUSTRATIONS FOR THIS BOOK. ADDITIONAL ART WAS PAINTED IN ACRYLIC ON PAPER.
THE TEXT WAS SET IN A FONT BASED ON CELIA JACOBS'S HANDWRITING.
LETTERING BY CELIA JACOBS
FLATTING BY REBECCA GOOD
DESIGN BY CELESTE KNUDSEN
24 25 26 27 28 COS 10 9 8 7 6 5 4 3 2 1

FIRST EDITION

TO MY FAMILY AND MIGRANT FARMWORKERS EVERYWHERE.

—F.J.

TO MY PARENTS, NANCY AND ROBERT, MY BROTHER, MARC, AND ALL FAMILIES WHO GO ABOVE AND BEYOND FOR EACH OTHER, WHETHER PARENTS OR CHILDREN.

—A.J.R.

TO MY PARENTS—THANKS FOR EVERYTHING.

—C.J.

CALIFORNIA
FRESNO
SANTA MARIA
MEXICALI
RANCHO BLANCO
GUADALAJARA
SAN LUIS OBISPO
GUADALUPE
SANTA MARIA

CALIFORNIA
FRESNO
FOWLER
SELMA
OROSI
VISALIA
FIVE POINTS
CORCORAN
BAKERSFIELD

UNDER the WIRE

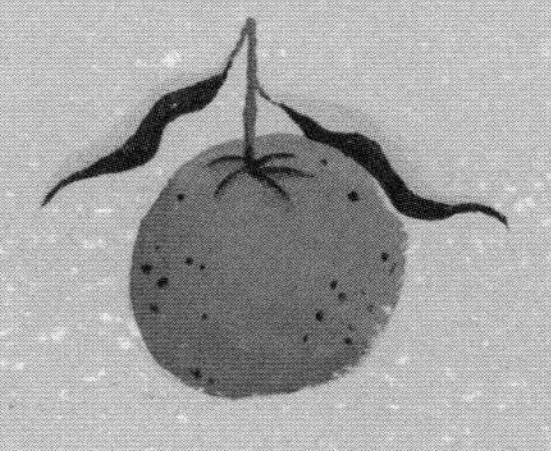

LA FRONTERA WAS A WORD I OFTEN HEARD WHEN I WAS A CHILD LIVING IN EL RANCHO BLANCO...
...A SMALL VILLAGE NESTLED ON BARREN, DRY HILLS SEVERAL MILES NORTH OF GUADALAJARA, MEXICO.

I HEARD IT FOR THE FIRST TIME BACK IN THE LATE 1940S...
...WHEN PAPÁ AND MAMÁ TOLD ME AND MY OLDER BROTHER, ROBERTO, THAT SOMEDAY WE'D TAKE A LONG TRIP NORTH TO CROSS LA FRONTERA, ENTER CALIFORNIA, AND LEAVE OUR POVERTY BEHIND.

I DID NOT KNOW EXACTLY WHAT CALIFORNIA WAS.
BUT PAPÁ'S EYES SPARKLED WHENEVER HE TALKED ABOUT IT WITH MAMÁ AND HIS FRIENDS.
ONCE WE CROSS LA FRONTERA, WE'LL MAKE A GOOD LIVING IN CALIFORNIA.

ROBERTO BECAME EXCITED EVERY TIME PAPÁ TALKED ABOUT THE TRIP TO CALIFORNIA.

ROBERTO DIDN'T LIKE EL RANCHO BLANCO, ESPECIALLY AFTER VISITING OUR OLDER COUSIN FITO IN GUADALAJARA.

FITO WORKED IN A TEQUILA FACTORY AND LIVED IN A TWO-BEDROOM HOUSE, WITH ELECTRICITY AND A WATER WELL.

HE DIDN'T HAVE TO GET UP AT FOUR IN THE MORNING ANYMORE TO MILK THE FIVE COWS BY HAND...
...NOR CARRY THE MILK IN A LARGE ALUMINUM CAN FOR SEVERAL MILES TO THE NEAREST ROAD...
...WHERE A TRUCK WOULD TRANSPORT IT TO TOWN TO SELL.
HE DIDN'T HAVE TO GO TO THE RIVER FOR WATER...
...OR SLEEP ON DIRT FLOORS OR USE CANDLES FOR LIGHT.

FROM THEN ON, THE ONLY THINGS ROBERTO LIKED ABOUT EL RANCHO BLANCO WERE HUNTING FOR CHICKEN EGGS AND ATTENDING CHURCH ON SUNDAYS.

DAYS LATER, WE PACKED OUR BELONGINGS IN A SUITCASE AND TOOK THE BUS TO GUADALAJARA TO CATCH THE TRAIN.

PAPÁ BOUGHT TICKETS ON A SECOND-CLASS TRAIN.
I HAD NEVER SEEN A TRAIN BEFORE.
BUMP
OOF
WOBBLE
SIT, PANCHITO.

IS THIS CALIFORNIA?
NO, MI'JO. WE'RE NOT THERE YET. WE HAVE MANY MORE HOURS TO GO.

WHAT'S CALIFORNIA LIKE?
I DON'T KNOW, BUT FITO TOLD ME THAT PEOPLE SWEEP MONEY OFF THE STREETS.
WHERE DID FITO GET THAT IDEA?
HE SAID CANTINFLAS SAID IT IN A MOVIE.
CANTINFLAS WAS JOKING, BUT IT'S TRUE THAT LIFE IS BETTER THERE.
I HOPE SO. DIOS LO QUIERA.

IS THIS CALIFORNIA?
¡OTRA VEZ LA BURRA AL TRIGO! I'LL TELL YOU WHEN WE GET THERE!
WE TRAVELED FOR TWO DAYS AND NIGHTS. DURING THE NIGHT, WE DIDN'T GET MUCH SLEEP.
THE WOODEN SEATS WERE HARD, AND THE TRAIN MADE LOUD NOISES, BLOWING ITS WHISTLE AND GRINDING ITS BRAKES.

MEXICALI
WE'RE ALMOST THERE.

THIS IS LA FRONTERA. ACROSS THE WIRE IS CALIFORNIA. WE HAVE TO CROSS TO THE OTHER SIDE OF THE FENCE WITHOUT BEING SEEN BY LA MIGRA.

LATE THAT NIGHT, WE WALKED FOR SEVERAL MILES AWAY FROM TOWN.
UNTIL PAPÁ PAUSED, LOOKED ALL AROUND TO MAKE SURE NO ONE COULD SEE US, AND HEADED TOWARD THE FENCE.

A FEW MINUTES LATER, WE WERE PICKED UP BY A WOMAN WHOM PAPÁ HAD CONTACTED IN MEXICALI.
SHE HAD PROMISED TO PICK US UP AND DRIVE US, FOR A FEE, TO A PLACE WHERE WE WOULD FIND WORK.

THE WOMAN DROVE ALL NIGHT.
AT DAWN WE REACHED A TENT LABOR CAMP ON THE OUTSKIRTS OF GUADALUPE, A SMALL TOWN ON THE COAST.

THIS IS THE PLACE I TOLD YOU ABOUT. HERE YOU'LL FIND WORK PICKING STRAWBERRIES.
WE HAD ONLY SEVEN DOLLARS LEFT.

THE FOREMAN HAS LEFT FOR THE DAY.
WE SPENT THAT NIGHT UNDERNEATH THE EUCALYPTUS TREES, PILING LEAVES TO SLEEP ON.

THE FOLLOWING MORNING, I WOKE TO THE SOUND OF A TRAIN WHISTLE.
SPEWING BLACK SMOKE, THE TRAIN PASSED, TRAVELING MUCH FASTER THAN THE ONE WE'D TAKEN FROM GUADALAJARA.

A WOMAN NAMED LUPE GORDILLO, FROM THE NEARBY CAMP, HAD STOPPED BY TO HELP.
SHE BROUGHT US A FEW GROCERIES AND INTRODUCED US TO THE CAMP FOREMAN.

YOU'RE LUCKY. THIS IS THE LAST TENT WE HAVE.

WHEN CAN WE START WORK?
IN TWO WEEKS.

THAT CAN'T BE! WE WERE TOLD WE'D FIND WORK RIGHT AWAY.
I AM SORRY. THE STRAWBERRIES WON'T BE READY FOR PICKING UNTIL THEN.
WE'LL MANAGE, VIEJO. ONCE WORK STARTS, WE'LL BE FINE.

DURING THE NEXT TWO WEEKS, MAMÁ COOKED OUTSIDE ON A MAKESHIFT STOVE.
WE ATE WILD VERDOLAGAS AND RABBIT AND BIRDS, WHICH PAPÁ HUNTED WITH A BORROWED RIFLE.

TO PASS THE TIME, ROBERTO AND I WOULD WATCH THE TRAINS GO BY BEHIND THE LABOR CAMP.
WE CRAWLED UNDER A BARBED-WIRE FENCE TO GET A CLOSER LOOK AT THEM AS THEY PASSED SEVERAL TIMES A DAY.
OUR FAVORITE TRAIN CAME BY EVERY DAY AT NOON.
IT HAD A DISTINCT WHISTLE FROM MILES AWAY. ROBERTO AND I CALLED IT THE NOON TRAIN.

OFTEN, WE WOULD GET THERE EARLY AND PLAY ON THE RAILROAD TRACKS WHILE WE WAITED FOR IT.

WE RAN, STRADDLING THE RAILS.

OR WALKED ON THEM AS FAST AS WE COULD TO SEE HOW FAR WE COULD GO WITHOUT FALLING OFF.

WE ALSO SAT ON THE RAILS TO FEEL THEM VIBRATE AS THE TRAIN APPROACHED.

AS DAYS WENT BY, WE COULD RECOGNIZE THE CONDUCTOR FROM AFAR.

I WONDER WHERE THE TRAIN COMES FROM. DO YOU KNOW, ROBERTO?
I HAVE BEEN WONDERING TOO, AND I THINK IT COMES FROM CALIFORNIA.

CALIFORNIA?! BUT WE ARE ALREADY IN CALIFORNIA!
I AM NOT SO SURE. REMEMBER WHAT FITO TOLD US HE SAW IN THE MOVIE ABOUT CALIFORNIA?
WHOOO
WHOO

THE FAMILIAR NOON TRAIN WHISTLE INTERRUPTED HIM.
THAT DAY, THE TRAIN SLOWED TO A CRAWL AND THE CONDUCTOR GENTLY DROPPED A BROWN BAG IN FRONT OF US.
FIC

IT WAS FULL OF ORANGES, APPLES, AND CANDY.
SEE, PANCHITO, THE TRAIN DOES COME FROM CALIFORNIA!

THE TRAIN SPED UP AND SOON LEFT US BEHIND.

WE FOLLOWED THE REAR OF THE TRAIN WITH OUR EYES UNTIL IT GOT SMALLER AND SMALLER... AND DISAPPEARED.

SOLEDAD

ONE COLD, EARLY MORNING IN BAKERSFIELD, PAPÁ PARKED THE CARCACHITA, OUR OLD JALOPY, AT ONE END OF THE COTTON FIELD.

HE, MAMÁ, AND ROBERTO CLIMBED OUT AND HEADED TOWARD THE OTHER END, WHERE THE PICKING STARTED.

AS USUAL, THEY LEFT ME ALONE TO TAKE CARE OF TRAMPITA, MY LITTLE BROTHER, WHO WAS SIX MONTHS OLD.

I HATED BEING LEFT BY MYSELF WITH HIM WHILE THEY WENT OFF TO PICK COTTON.
I WATCHED THEM UNTIL I COULD NO LONGER TELL THEM APART FROM THE OTHER PICKERS.

ONCE I LOST SIGHT OF THEM, I FELT THE SAME PAIN IN MY CHEST THAT I ALWAYS FELT WHENEVER THEY LEFT TRAMPITA AND ME ALONE.

AFTER SEVERAL LONG HOURS, I CLIMBED ONTO THE ROOF OF THE CAR AGAIN.

FINALLY I SAW PAPÁ, MAMÁ, AND ROBERTO RETURNING, AND MY HEART STARTED RACING.

MAMÁ PULLED OUT THE TACOS SHE HAD PREPARED AT DAWN THAT MORNING.

PAPÁ ATE QUICKLY BECAUSE HE DID NOT WANT TO LOSE TIME FROM WORK.

ROBERTO AND I ATE SLOWLY, TRYING TO MAKE LUNCHTIME LAST A BIT LONGER.

MAMÁ NURSED TRAMPITA, CHANGED HIS DIAPER, THEN LAID HIM DOWN FOR A NAP AND KISSED HIM GENTLY ON HIS FOREHEAD AS HE FELL ASLEEP.

PAPÁ PICKED UP HIS COTTON SACK, SIGNALING THAT IT WAS TIME TO GO BACK TO WORK.
IF I LEARN TO PICK, PAPÁ WILL LET ME GO WITH THEM AND I WON'T BE LEFT ALONE ANYMORE!

AFTER CHECKING ON TRAMPITA...

...I QUIETLY WALKED OVER TO THE ROW NEAREST THE CAR AND PICKED COTTON FOR THE FIRST TIME.

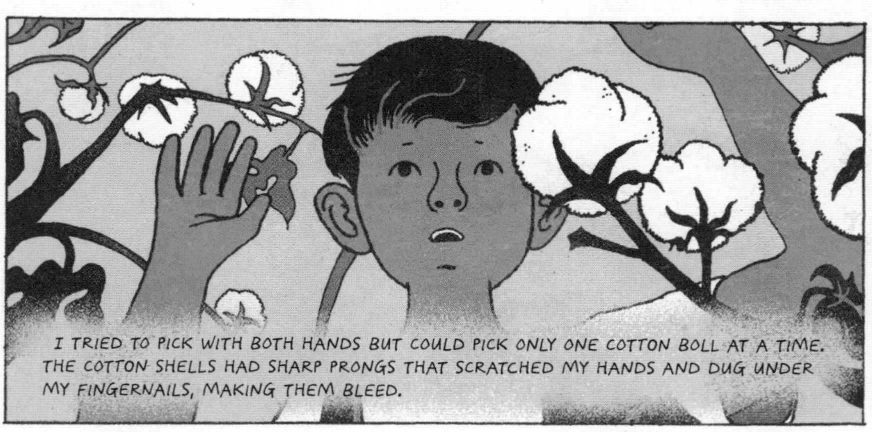
I TRIED TO PICK WITH BOTH HANDS BUT COULD PICK ONLY ONE COTTON BOLL AT A TIME. THE COTTON SHELLS HAD SHARP PRONGS THAT SCRATCHED MY HANDS AND DUG UNDER MY FINGERNAILS, MAKING THEM BLEED.

I HAD TROUBLE REACHING THE COTTON BOLLS AT THE VERY TOP OF THE TALL PLANTS.

SO I LEANED AGAINST THE PLANTS AND PUSHED THEM OVER WITH MY BODY UNTIL THEY TOUCHED THE GROUND, BUT THEY WHIPPED ME IN THE FACE IF I MOVED TOO SLOWLY.

AT THE END OF THE DAY, I WAS TIRED AND DISAPPOINTED. I HAD NOT PICKED AS MUCH COTTON AS I HAD WANTED TO.
THE PILE WAS ONLY ABOUT TWO FEET HIGH.

THEN I REMEMBERED PAPÁ SAYING WE GOT PAID THREE CENTS A POUND.
SO I MIXED DIRT CLODS WITH THE COTTON TO MAKE IT WEIGH MORE.

AT DUSK, PAPÁ, MAMÁ, AND ROBERTO FINALLY RETURNED. I WAS ABOUT TO TELL THEM MY SURPRISE...
HOW IS TRAMPITA?!

I HAD BEEN SO BUSY LEARNING HOW TO PICK COTTON THAT I HAD FORGOTTEN ALL ABOUT TRAMPITA.
TIRED FROM CRYING, HE HAD FALLEN ASLEEP AFTER SOILING HIMSELF AND BREAKING THE BOTTLE OF MILK.

I TOLD YOU TO TAKE CARE OF TRAMPITA!
BUT LOOK WHAT I DID.

PAPÁ'S GRIN QUICKLY TURNED INTO A FROWN WHEN HE DISCOVERED THE DIRT CLODS.
YOU SHOULD BE ASHAMED. WE COULD BE FIRED FOR THIS.
YOUR JOB IS TO TAKE CARE OF TRAMPITA. IS THAT CLEAR?
SÍ, PAPÁ.

SOMEDAY, I WILL GET TO GO PICK COTTON WITH YOU, ROBERTO. THEN I WON'T BE LEFT ALONE.

INSIDE OUT

I WISHED I HAD NOT ASKED HIM WHAT IT WOULD BE LIKE, BUT ROBERTO WAS THE ONLY ONE IN OUR FAMILY, INCLUDING MAMÁ AND PAPÁ, WHO HAD EVER ATTENDED SCHOOL.
I REMEMBER BEING HIT ON THE WRISTS WITH A TWELVE-INCH RULER...

...BECAUSE I DID NOT FOLLOW DIRECTIONS IN CLASS. BUT HOW COULD I? THE TEACHER GAVE THEM IN ENGLISH.

SO WHAT DID YOU DO?
I ALWAYS GUESSED WHAT SHE WANTED ME TO DO.
AND WHEN SHE DID NOT USE THE RULER ON ME, I KNEW I GUESSED RIGHT.
SOME OF THE KIDS MADE FUN OF ME WHEN I GOT ENGLISH WRONG.
I HAD TO REPEAT FIRST GRADE.

LIKE ROBERTO, I DID NOT SPEAK OR UNDERSTAND ENGLISH. AND I FELT ANXIOUS.
BUT I WAS EXCITED TO GO TO SCHOOL IN SANTA MARIA.
IT WAS LATE JANUARY AND WE HAD JUST RETURNED FROM PICKING COTTON IN CORCORAN.

ON MY FIRST DAY OF SCHOOL, I DRESSED IN OVERALLS, WHICH I HATED BECAUSE THEY HAD SUSPENDERS, AND A FLANNEL SHIRT MAMÁ HAD BOUGHT AT THE GOODWILL STORE.
AS I PUT ON MY CAP, ROBERTO REMINDED ME THAT IT WAS BAD MANNERS TO WEAR A HAT INDOORS.
I THOUGHT OF LEAVING IT AT HOME SO THAT I WOULD NOT FORGET TO TAKE IT OFF IN CLASS, BUT I DECIDED TO WEAR IT.
PAPÁ ALWAYS WORE A CAP, AND I DID NOT FEEL COMPLETELY DRESSED FOR SCHOOL WITHOUT IT.

PAPÁ HAD ALREADY LEFT TO LOOK FOR WORK, EITHER TOPPING CARROTS OR THINNING LETTUCE.

MAMÁ STAYED HOME TO TAKE CARE OF TRAMPITA AND TO REST BECAUSE SHE WAS EXPECTING ANOTHER BABY.

WHEN THE SCHOOL BUS ARRIVED, ROBERTO AND I CLIMBED ON AND SAT TOGETHER.

I WATCHED ENDLESS ROWS OF LETTUCE AND CAULIFLOWER WHIZ BY.

THE FURROWS CAME UP TO THE TWO-LANE ROAD AND LOOKED LIKE GIANT LEGS RUNNING ALONGSIDE US.

THE BUS MADE SEVERAL STOPS TO PICK UP KIDS, AND WITH EACH STOP, THE NOISE INSIDE GOT LOUDER.
I DID NOT KNOW WHAT ANYONE WAS SAYING.

BY THE TIME WE GOT TO MAIN STREET SCHOOL, THE BUS WAS PACKED.

WE MET THE PRINCIPAL, MR. SIMS.

HE PATIENTLY LISTENED AS ROBERTO, USING THE LITTLE ENGLISH HE KNEW, MANAGED TO ENROLL ME IN FIRST GRADE.
FRANCISCO

MR. SIMS WALKED ME TO MY CLASSROOM. I LIKED IT AS SOON AS I SAW IT.
UNLIKE OUR TENT, IT HAD WOODEN FLOORS, ELECTRIC LIGHTS, AND HEAT.

MR. SIMS INTRODUCED ME TO MY TEACHER, MISS SCALAPINO.
FRANCISCO
FRANCISCO

"FRANCISCO" WAS THE ONLY WORD I UNDERSTOOD.
, FRANCISCO!

AFTER MR. SIMS LEFT, MISS SCALAPINO SHOWED ME TO MY DESK, WHICH WAS AT THE END OF THE ROW CLOSEST TO THE WINDOWS.
THERE WERE NO OTHER KIDS IN THE ROOM YET.

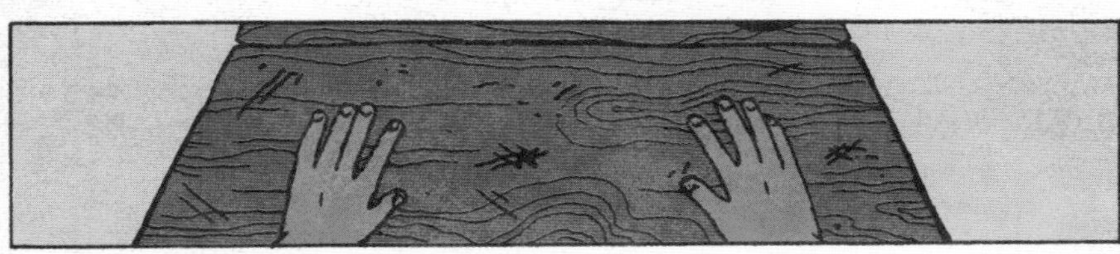

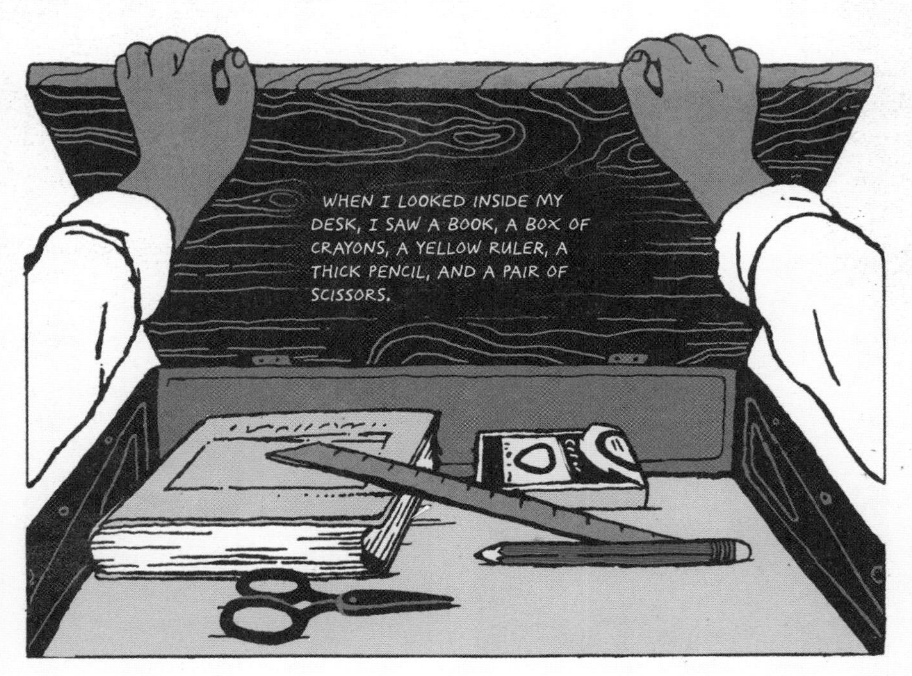
WHEN I LOOKED INSIDE MY DESK, I SAW A BOOK, A BOX OF CRAYONS, A YELLOW RULER, A THICK PENCIL, AND A PAIR OF SCISSORS.

UNDER THE WINDOWS WAS A DARK WOODEN COUNTER THE LENGTH OF THE ROOM.
ON TOP OF IT, RIGHT NEXT TO MY DESK, WAS A CATERPILLAR IN A LARGE JAR.
HE LOOKED JUST LIKE THE ONES I HAD SEEN IN THE FIELDS.
HE WAS YELLOWISH GREEN WITH BLACK BANDS, AND HE MOVED VERY SLOWLY, WITHOUT MAKING ANY SOUND.

RRIIINN

SOON, OTHER KIDS WALKED QUIETLY INTO THE ROOM AND TOOK THEIR SEATS.
SOME OF THEM LOOKED AT ME AND GIGGLED.

I LOOKED AT THE CATERPILLAR IN THE JAR EVERY TIME SOMEONE LOOKED AT ME.

MISS SCALAPINO STARTED SPEAKING TO THE CLASS...
...I DID NOT UNDERSTAND A WORD SHE WAS SAYING. THE MORE SHE SPOKE, THE MORE ANXIOUS I BECAME.

BY THE END OF THE DAY, I WAS VERY TIRED OF HEARING MISS SCALAPINO TALK. THE SOUNDS HAD MADE NO SENSE TO ME.
I THOUGHT THAT PERHAPS BY PAYING CLOSE ATTENTION, I WOULD BEGIN TO UNDERSTAND, BUT THAT DIDN'T HAPPEN.
FOR DAYS I GOT HEADACHES FROM TRYING TO LISTEN, UNTIL I LEARNED A WAY OUT.

WHEN MY HEAD BEGAN TO HURT, I LET MY MIND WANDER.
SOMETIMES I IMAGINED MYSELF FLYING OUT OF THE CLASSROOM AND LANDING NEXT TO PAPÁ AND SURPRISING HIM.

BUT WHEN I DAYDREAMED, I CONTINUED TO LOOK AT THE TEACHER AND PRETEND I WAS PAYING ATTENTION...
...BECAUSE PAPÁ HAD TOLD ME THAT IT WAS DISRESPECTFUL NOT TO PAY ATTENTION, ESPECIALLY TO GROWNUPS.

IT WAS EASIER WHEN MISS SCALAPINO READ TO THE CLASS FROM A BOOK WITH ILLUSTRATIONS.
I WOULD MAKE UP MY OWN STORIES IN SPANISH, BASED ON THE PICTURES.
STILL, I WISHED I COULD UNDERSTAND WHAT SHE WAS READING.

IN TIME I LEARNED SOME OF MY CLASSMATES' NAMES.
THE ONE I HEARD THE MOST AND THEREFORE LEARNED FIRST WAS CURTIS.
CURTIS WAS THE BIGGEST, STRONGEST, AND MOST POPULAR KID IN THE CLASS.
EVERYONE WANTED TO BE HIS FRIEND AND TO PLAY WITH HIM.
HE WAS ALWAYS CHOSEN AS CAPTAIN WHEN THE KIDS FORMED TEAMS.

SINCE I WAS THE SMALLEST AND DID NOT KNOW ENGLISH, I WAS ALWAYS CHOSEN LAST.

I PREFERRED TO HANG AROUND ARTHUR, ONE OF THE BOYS WHO KNEW A LITTLE SPANISH.

DURING RECESS, HE AND I WOULD PLAY ON THE SWINGS.

I PRETENDED TO BE A MEXICAN MOVIE STAR, LIKE JORGE NEGRETE OR PEDRO INFANTE...

...RIDING A HORSE AND SINGING THE CORRIDOS WE OFTEN HEARD ON THE CAR RADIO.
I WOULD SING THE SONGS TO ARTHUR AS WE SWUNG BACK AND FORTH, GOING AS HIGH AS WE COULD. UNTIL ONE DAY MISS SCALAPINO OVERHEARD ME.

NO!
ENGLISH...ENGLISH...
ENGLISH.
ENGLISH!

ARTHUR BEGAN TO AVOID ME WHENEVER SHE WAS AROUND.

SO, OFTEN DURING RECESS, I STARTED STAYING IN WITH THE CATERPILLAR.
SOMETIMES IT WAS HARD TO SPOT HIM IN THE JAR BECAUSE HE BLENDED IN WITH THE GREEN LEAVES AND TWIGS.

EVERY DAY I WOULD BRING HIM LEAVES FROM THE PEPPER AND CYPRESS TREES THAT GREW ON THE PLAYGROUND.

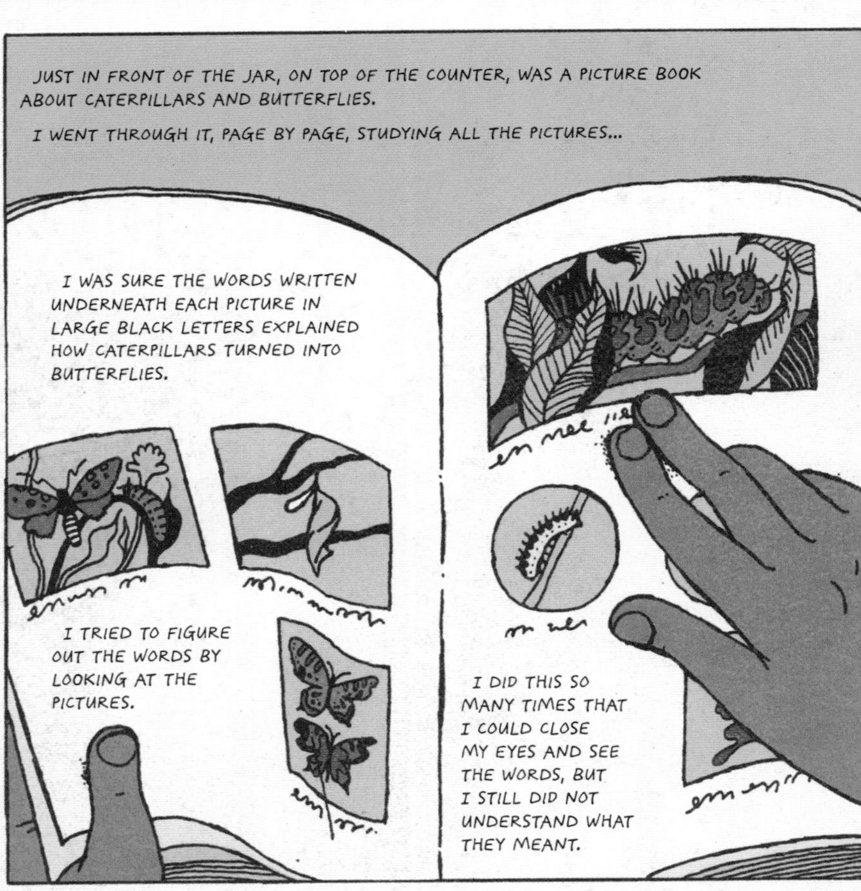
JUST IN FRONT OF THE JAR, ON TOP OF THE COUNTER, WAS A PICTURE BOOK ABOUT CATERPILLARS AND BUTTERFLIES.
I WENT THROUGH IT, PAGE BY PAGE, STUDYING ALL THE PICTURES...
I WAS SURE THE WORDS WRITTEN UNDERNEATH EACH PICTURE IN LARGE BLACK LETTERS EXPLAINED HOW CATERPILLARS TURNED INTO BUTTERFLIES.
I TRIED TO FIGURE OUT THE WORDS BY LOOKING AT THE PICTURES.
I DID THIS SO MANY TIMES THAT I COULD CLOSE MY EYES AND SEE THE WORDS, BUT I STILL DID NOT UNDERSTAND WHAT THEY MEANT.

MY FAVORITE TIME IN SCHOOL WAS WHEN WE WOULD DO ART EVERY AFTERNOON.
SINCE I DID NOT UNDERSTAND MISS SCALAPINO WHEN SHE EXPLAINED THE LESSONS, SHE LET ME DO WHAT I WANTED.

I DREW ALL KINDS OF ANIMALS BUT MOSTLY BIRDS AND BUTTERFLIES.
I SKETCHED THEM IN PENCIL AND THEN COLORED THEM USING EVERY COLOR IN MY CRAYON BOX.

MISS SCALAPINO EVEN TACKED UP ONE OF MY DRAWINGS ON THE BOARD FOR EVERYONE TO SEE.

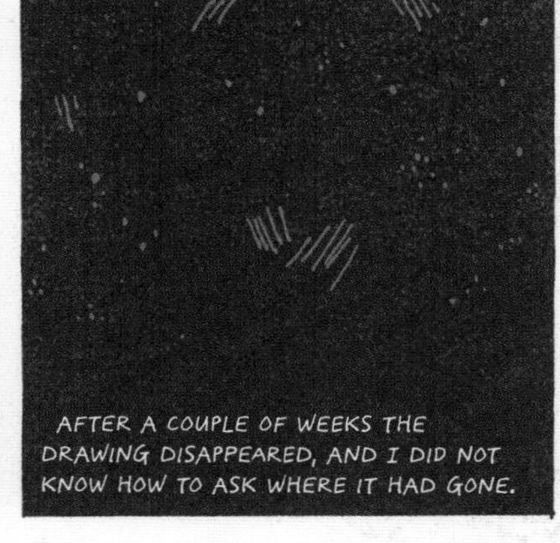
AFTER A COUPLE OF WEEKS THE DRAWING DISAPPEARED, AND I DID NOT KNOW HOW TO ASK WHERE IT HAD GONE.

ONE COLD MONDAY MORNING, DURING RECESS, I WAS THE ONLY KID ON THE PLAYGROUND WITHOUT A JACKET.
MR. SIMS MUST HAVE NOTICED.

THAT AFTERNOON, AFTER SCHOOL, HE TOOK ME TO HIS OFFICE AND PULLED OUT A GREEN JACKET FROM A LARGE CARDBOARD BOX THAT WAS FULL OF USED CLOTHES AND TOYS.

THE COAT SMELLED LIKE GRAHAM CRACKERS. I PUT IT ON, BUT IT WAS TOO BIG.

I TOOK THE JACKET HOME AND SHOWED IT OFF TO MY PARENTS. THEY SMILED.
I LIKED IT BECAUSE IT WAS GREEN AND IT HID MY SUSPENDERS.

THE NEXT DAY, I WAS ON THE PLAYGROUND, WEARING MY NEW JACKET AND WAITING FOR THE FIRST BELL TO RING...

...WHEN I SAW CURTIS COMING AT ME LIKE AN ANGRY BULL.
I DID NOT UNDERSTAND HIM, BUT I KNEW IT HAD SOMETHING TO DO WITH THE JACKET, WHICH I STUBBORNLY HELD ON TO.

WHAM
POP...

RRRIIPP

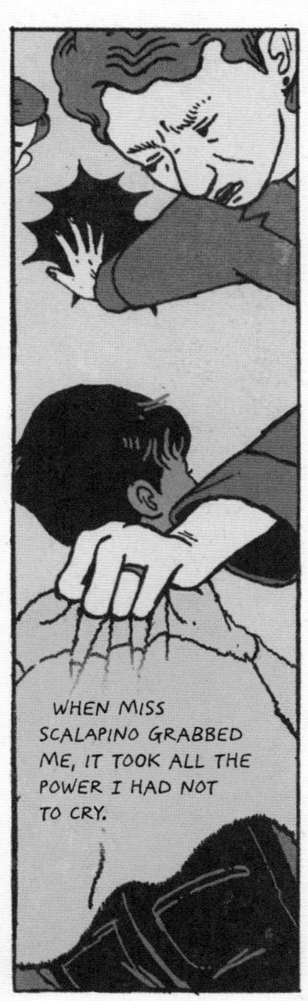
WHEN MISS SCALAPINO GRABBED ME, IT TOOK ALL THE POWER I HAD NOT TO CRY.

ARTHUR WALKED WITH ME INTO THE CLASSROOM.
CURTIS SAYS HE LOST THE JACKET AT THE BEGINNING OF THE YEAR.

ARTHUR ALSO SAID THE TEACHER TOLD CURTIS AND ME THAT WE HAD TO SIT ON THE BENCH DURING RECESS FOR THE REST OF THE WEEK.

I DID NOT SEE THE JACKET AGAIN. CURTIS GOT IT BUT I NEVER SAW HIM WEAR IT.

FOR THE REST OF THAT DAY, I LAID MY HEAD ON TOP OF MY DESK AND CLOSED MY EYES.
MISS SCALAPINO MUST HAVE THOUGHT I WAS ASLEEP, BECAUSE SHE LEFT ME ALONE, EVEN WHEN IT WAS TIME FOR RECESS.

ONCE THE ROOM WAS QUIET, I SLOWLY OPENED MY EYES.
WHEN I LOOKED AT THE JAR, I COULDN'T SEE THE CATERPILLAR. NOT EVEN WHEN I GENTLY STIRRED THE LEAVES, WHICH WAS WHEN I DISCOVERED...

...THE CATERPILLAR HAD SPUN ITSELF INTO A COCOON.
I IMAGINED IT ASLEEP AND PEACEFUL.

PAPÁ AND MAMÁ DID NOT KNOW HOW TO READ, BUT THEY DID NOT HAVE TO.
AS SOON AS THEY SAW MY SWOLLEN UPPER LIP AND THE SCRATCHES ON MY CHEEK, THEY KNEW WHAT THE NOTE SAID.
WHEN I TOLD THEM WHAT HAD HAPPENED, THEY WERE UPSET BUT RELIEVED THAT I HAD NOT DISRESPECTED THE TEACHER.

AS DAYS WENT BY, I SLOWLY BEGAN TO GET OVER WHAT HAD HAPPENED, AND ONCE I BEGAN TO PICK UP SOME ENGLISH WORDS, I FELT MORE COMFORTABLE IN CLASS.
FRANCISCO!
ON WEDNESDAY, MARCH 19, MISS SCALAPINO CALLED FOR EVERYONE'S ATTENTION AND TOOK ME BY SURPRISE.
THANK YOU!
I HAD RECEIVED FIRST PLACE FOR MY DRAWING.

LATER THAT AFTERNOON, I TURNED OVER THE JAR, TRYING TO SEE THE COCOON.
WE ALL STOOD THERE WATCHING AS THE COCOON BEGAN TO CRACK OPEN.
LOOK! LOOK!

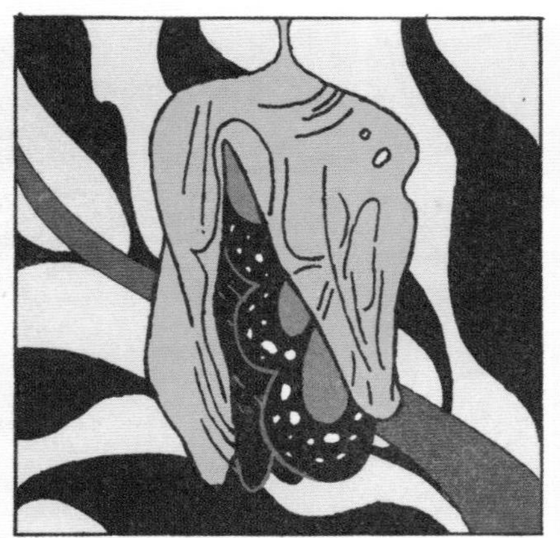

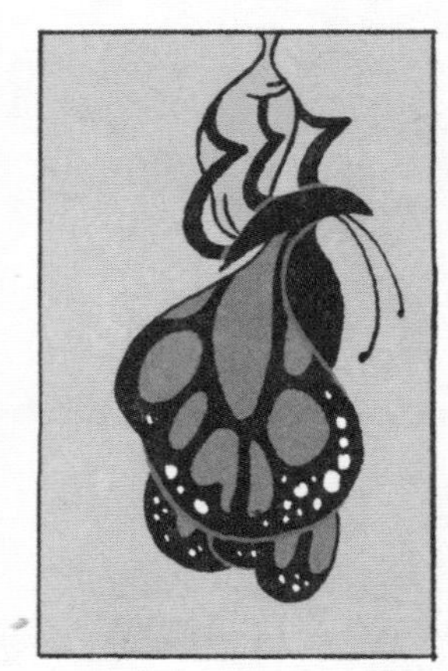

AT THE END OF THE DAY, MISS SCALAPINO TOOK THE CLASS OUTSIDE TO THE PLAYGROUND.

WHY DON'T YOU OPEN THE JAR, FRANCISCO?

CURTIS REALLY
LIKES IT, FRANCISCO.

¿CÓMO SE DICE "ES TUYO" EN INGLÉS?

"IT'S YOURS."

IT'S YOURS, CURTIS.

MIRACLE in TENT CITY

WE CALLED IT TENT CITY. EVERYBODY CALLED IT TENT CITY, ALTHOUGH IT WAS NEITHER A CITY NOR A TOWN.
IT WAS A FARM-WORKER LABOR CAMP OWNED BY SHEEHEY STRAWBERRY FARMS.
TENT CITY HAD NO ADDRESS; IT WAS SIMPLY KNOWN AS "RURAL SANTA MARIA."

IT WAS ON MAIN STREET, ABOUT TEN MILES EAST OF THE CENTER OF SANTA MARIA.
A MILE NORTH OF TENT CITY WAS THE CITY DUMP.
MANY OF THE RESIDENTS WERE SINGLE MEN, MOST OF WHOM, LIKE US, HAD CROSSED THE BORDER ILLEGALLY.
THERE WERE A FEW SINGLE WOMEN AND A FEW FAMILIES, ALL MEXICAN.

WHEN MAMÁ WAS A FEW WEEKS AWAY FROM GIVING BIRTH TO ANOTHER BABY, SHE COULD NO LONGER JOIN PAPÁ IN THE FIELDS.
TO MAKE ENDS MEET, SHE COOKED FOR TWENTY FARM WORKERS WHO LIVED IN TENT CITY.

SHE WOULD MAKE THEIR LUNCHES AND HAVE SUPPER READY FOR THEM, GETTING UP AT FOUR O'CLOCK EVERY MORNING, SEVEN DAYS A WEEK, TO MAKE THE TORTILLAS FOR BOTH MEALS.

ON WEEKENDS, ROBERTO AND I HELPED HER.

WE ROLLED THE TACOS, WRAPPED THEM IN WAX PAPER, AND DELIVERED THEM TO THE WORKERS, WHO WERE GIVEN HALF AN HOUR FOR LUNCH.

WE CLEANED THE POTS AND WASHED THE DISHES IN A LARGE ALUMINUM TUB.

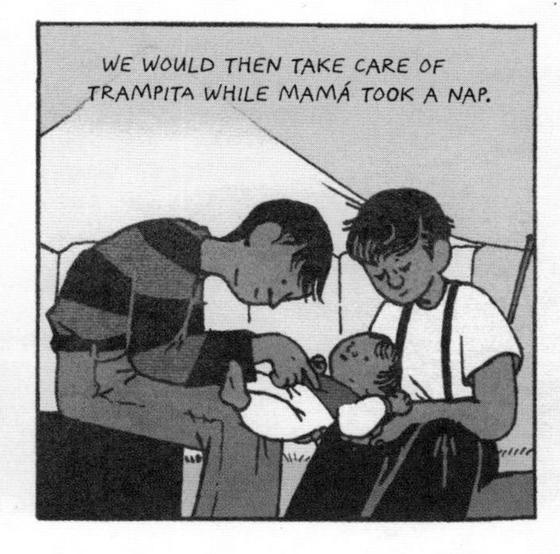
WE WOULD THEN TAKE CARE OF TRAMPITA WHILE MAMÁ TOOK A NAP.

TO GET EVERYTHING READY FOR THE NEW BABY, MAMÁ ASKED PAPÁ TO SEAL THE BASE OF THE TENT BY PILING EXTRA DIRT, SIX INCHES HIGH, ALL AROUND THE OUTSIDE TO FEND OFF SNAKES.

WHEN PAPÁ HAD FINISHED, MAMÁ PLEADED WITH HIM TO BUILD A FLOOR. EVERY EVENING, HE SENT ROBERTO AND ME TO THE CITY DUMP TO LOOK FOR DISCARDED LUMBER.

OUR TRIPS TO THE DUMP WERE ALWAYS AN ADVENTURE. WE WOULD WAIT UNTIL DUSK, AFTER THE DUMP CARETAKER HAD LEFT.

ONE EVENING, THE CARETAKER HID BEHIND ONE OF THE MOUNDS OF RUBBISH.
HE CHASED US AWAY, YELLING AND CURSING IN BROKEN SPANISH.

WE WERE SCARED AND WENT HOME EMPTY-HANDED.
BUT WE WENT BACK SEVERAL MORE TIMES UNTIL WE GOT ENOUGH LUMBER TO COMPLETE MAMÁ'S FLOOR.

WE ALSO FOUND PIECES OF LINOLEUM TO LAY OVER THE WOOD TO COVER THE HOLES AND SLIVERS. A LARGE WOODEN BOX, WITH A GREEN ARMY BLANKET AND A WHITE FLOUR SACK FOR A PILLOW, BECAME THE CRIB FOR THE NEW BABY.

MAMÁ MADE SURE THE ENTRANCE TO OUR TENT WAS ALWAYS CLOSED TO KEEP OUT THE SMOKE AND ODOR FROM THE CAMP'S GARBAGE DUMP, WHICH WAS A BIG HOLE IN THE GROUND. WE SET FIRE TO IT PERIODICALLY TO BURN THE TRASH.
ON WINDY DAYS, THE FOUL SMELL OF THE SANTA MARIA DUMP COMPETED WITH THE STENCH OF THE TENT CITY DUMP.

THE OLDER KIDS WOULD KILL SNAKES AND THROW THEM INTO THE GARBAGE HOLE WHEN IT WAS BURNING.
I COULD NOT FIGURE OUT WHY THE SNAKES TWISTED AND TURNED IN THE FIRE AFTER THEY WERE DEAD.
IT WAS AS THOUGH THE FIRE BROUGHT THEM BACK TO LIFE.

ONCE, TRAMPITA GOT TOO CLOSE TO THE GARBAGE HOLE AND FELL IN.

LUCKILY IT WAS NOT BURNING.

FROM THEN ON, PAPÁ DID NOT LET US PLAY NEAR THE HOLE.

WHEN THE BABY WAS FINALLY BORN, ROBERTO, TRAMPITA, AND I WERE EXCITED TO SEE HIM.

WE HAD WORKED SO HARD TO GET THINGS READY FOR HIM.

PAPÁ AND MAMÁ NAMED HIM JUAN MANUEL, BUT WE ALL CALLED HIM TORITO, OR "LITTLE BULL," BECAUSE HE WEIGHED TEN POUNDS AT BIRTH.

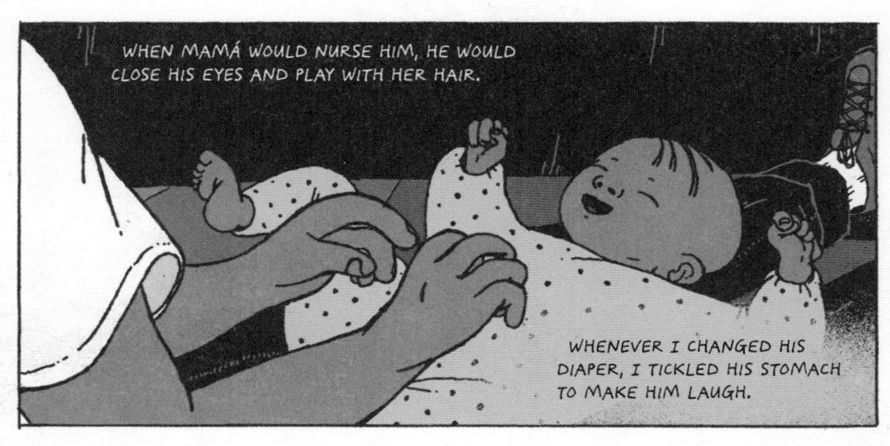
WHEN MAMÁ WOULD NURSE HIM, HE WOULD CLOSE HIS EYES AND PLAY WITH HER HAIR.
WHENEVER I CHANGED HIS DIAPER, I TICKLED HIS STOMACH TO MAKE HIM LAUGH.

TORITO HELPED ME FORGET ABOUT THE REPORT CARD I HAD RECEIVED IN EARLY JUNE, A FEW DAYS BEFORE HE WAS BORN.
MISS SCALAPINO SAID I HAD TO REPEAT FIRST GRADE BECAUSE I DID NOT KNOW ENGLISH WELL ENOUGH.

ABOUT TWO MONTHS AFTER HE WAS BORN, TORITO GOT SICK. HE CRIED OFF AND ON ALL DURING THE NIGHT.

THE NEXT MORNING WHEN I TICKLED HIM, HE DID NOT EVEN SMILE. HE LOOKED PALE.
I THINK TORITO HAS A FEVER. PLEASE LOOK AFTER HIM WHILE ROBERTO AND I PREPARE THE LUNCHES.

THAT AFTERNOON, WE HAD TO CHANGE HIM OFTEN.
THE FOLLOWING DAY, THE ALUMINUM TUB WAS ALMOST FULL OF TERRIBLE-SMELLING SOILED DIAPERS.

TO RINSE THEM, I FILLED A BUCKET FROM THE FAUCET IN THE MIDDLE OF THE CAMP.

MAMÁ BATHED TORITO IN COLD WATER SEVERAL TIMES A DAY, TRYING TO BRING DOWN HIS FEVER.
BUT IT DID NOT DO ANY GOOD.

IN THE EVENINGS, WE PRAYED FOR HIM IN FRONT OF A FADED PICTURE OF THE VIRGEN DE GUADALUPE.

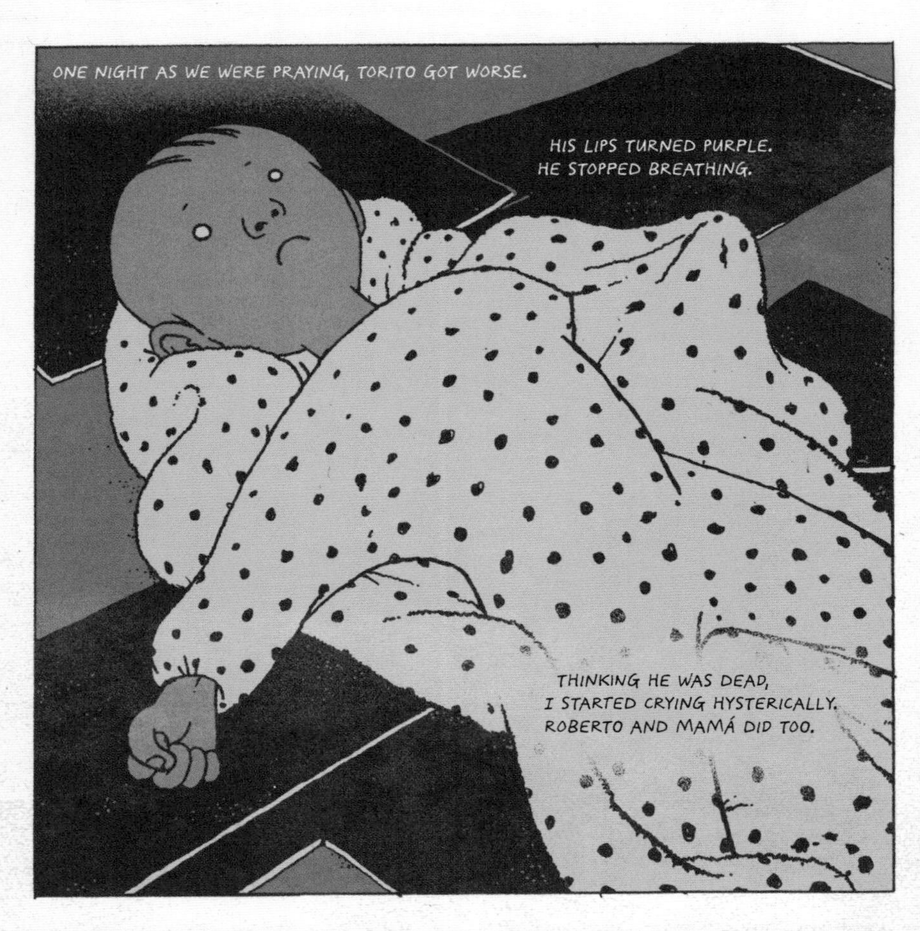
ONE NIGHT AS WE WERE PRAYING, TORITO GOT WORSE.
HIS LIPS TURNED PURPLE.
HE STOPPED BREATHING.
THINKING HE WAS DEAD,
I STARTED CRYING HYSTERICALLY.
ROBERTO AND MAMÁ DID TOO.

SHE PICKED HIM UP FROM THE BOX
AND HELD HIM TIGHTLY TO HER CHEST.
PLEASE, GOD,
DON'T TAKE HIM
AWAY—PLEASE!

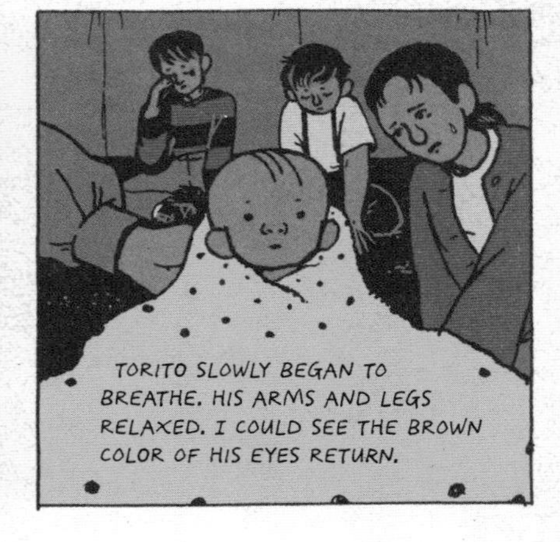
TORITO SLOWLY BEGAN TO
BREATHE. HIS ARMS AND LEGS
RELAXED. I COULD SEE THE BROWN
COLOR OF HIS EYES RETURN.

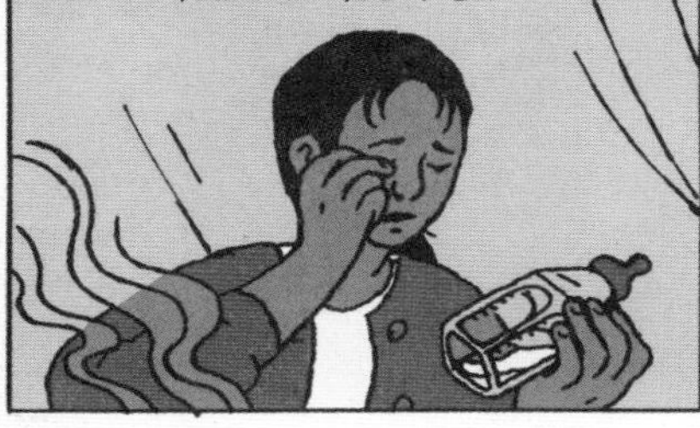
NO ONE SLEPT WELL THAT NIGHT. THE NEXT MORNING, MAMÁ'S EYES WERE PUFFY AND RED.
SHE TRIED TO NURSE TORITO, BUT SHE WAS NOT PRODUCING ENOUGH MILK SO SHE PREPARED HIM A BOTTLE.

BY THE AFTERNOON, SHE COULD HARDLY KEEP HER HEAD UP.

WHAAAAAA
LEAP
WILL YOU CLEAN THE BEANS FOR SUPPER?

ALL WE HAVE TONIGHT: FRIJOLES DE LA OLLA. I HOPE THE BOARDERS WON'T MIND.
THEY WON'T.

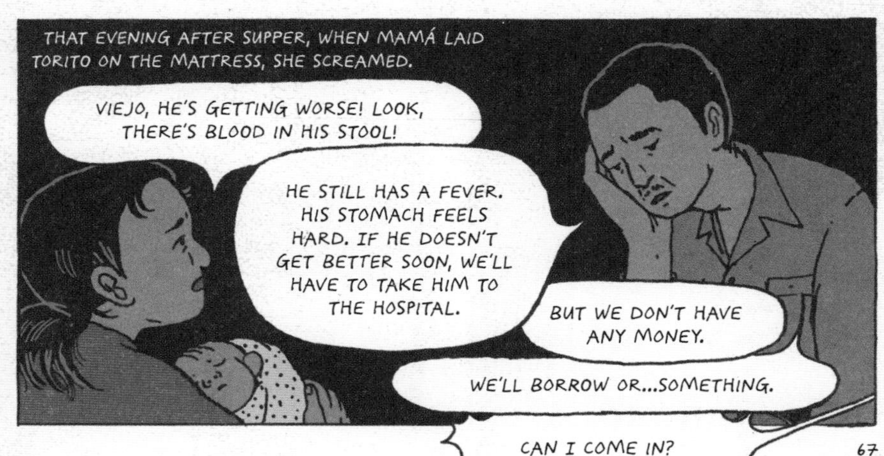
THAT EVENING AFTER SUPPER, WHEN MAMÁ LAID TORITO ON THE MATTRESS, SHE SCREAMED.
VIEJO, HE'S GETTING WORSE! LOOK, THERE'S BLOOD IN HIS STOOL!
HE STILL HAS A FEVER. HIS STOMACH FEELS HARD. IF HE DOESN'T GET BETTER SOON, WE'LL HAVE TO TAKE HIM TO THE HOSPITAL.
BUT WE DON'T HAVE ANY MONEY.
WE'LL BORROW OR...SOMETHING.
CAN I COME IN?

DOÑA MARÍA WAS KNOWN AS LA CURANDERA BECAUSE SHE HAD A GIFT FOR CURING PEOPLE USING HERBS AND CHANTS.

I'VE BEEN HEARING YOUR BABY CRY. WHAT'S WRONG WITH HIM?
WE DON'T KNOW.

COULD IT BE THE EVIL EYE? HE'S A VERY HANDSOME CHILD.

¿EL MAL DE OJO? NO, I THINK IT'S HIS STOMACH. IT'S HARD AS A ROCK. FEEL IT.

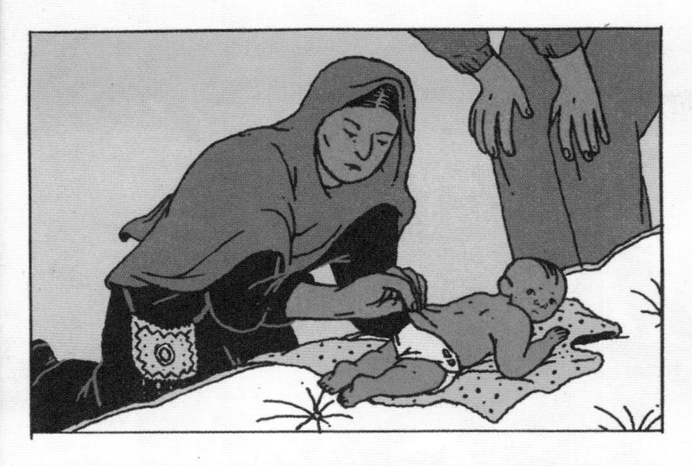

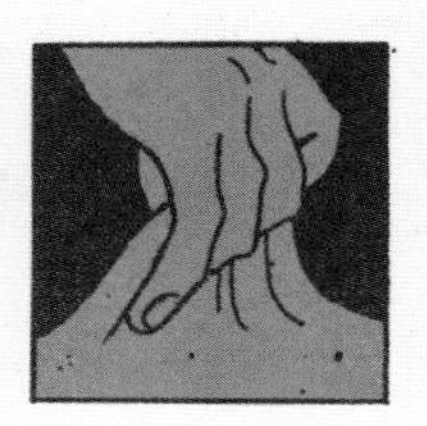

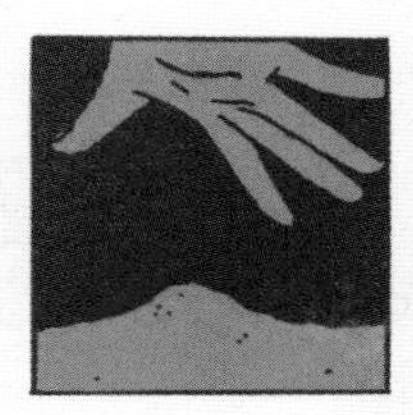

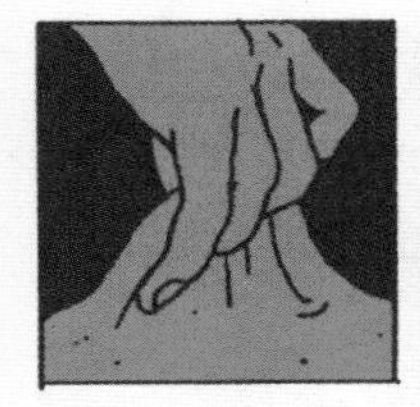

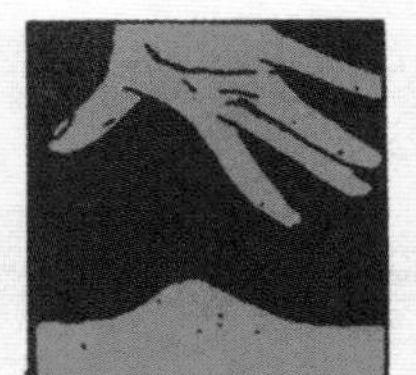

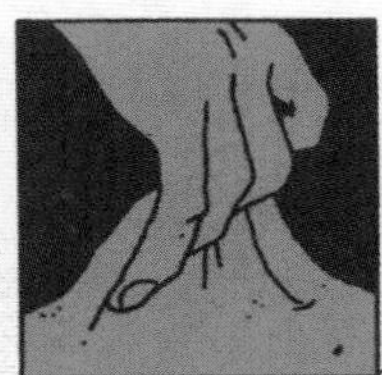

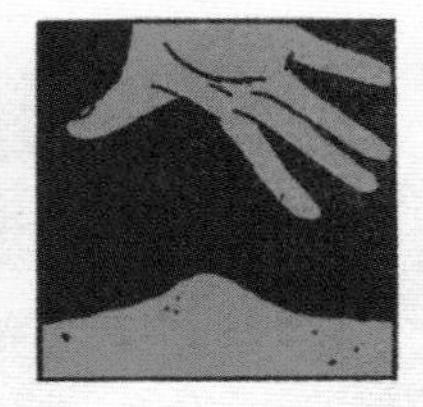

BRING ME THREE EGGS.

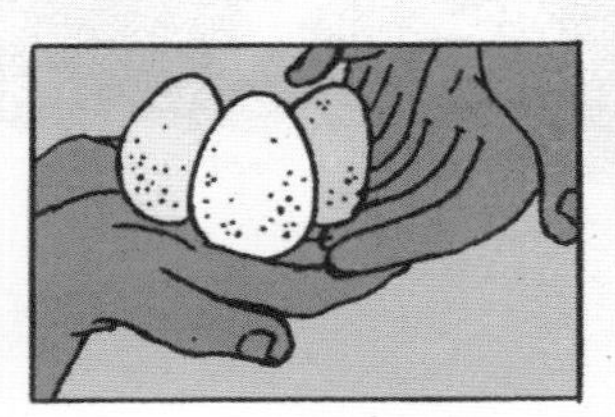

THE EGGS WILL DRAW OUT HIS SICKNESS.

MOMENTS LATER, TORITO STARTED MOANING. THEN HE SUDDENLY STOPPED AND BECAME STIFF AS A BOARD.

¡VIEJA, VÁMONOS AL HOSPITAL!

I WILL NEVER SEE HIM AGAIN.

IS HE DEAD?
NO, PANCHITO—CALM DOWN. WE LEFT HIM AT THE HOSPITAL.
IS HE GOING...TO DIE?
NO, HE ISN'T. GOD WON'T LET HIM. YOU'LL SEE.

EARLY TOMORROW MORNING, I AM GOING TO DRIVE YOU TO WORK.
THIS WAS STRANGE BECAUSE PAPÁ ALWAYS TOOK THE CAR TO GO PICK STRAWBERRIES.
WHEN THEY LEFT IN THE MORNING, ROBERTO AND I DID NOT SAY A WORD TO EACH OTHER, BUT EACH OF US KNEW WHAT THE OTHER WAS THINKING.

AROUND ELEVEN O'CLOCK, MAMÁ RETURNED.
WHERE WERE YOU? I WANT TO GO SEE TORITO.
ONLY IF GOD WILLS IT. TORITO HAS A RARE DISEASE. IT MAY BE CONTAGIOUS. THAT'S WHY YOU CAN'T SEE HIM.
BUT YOU WENT TO SEE HIM THIS MORNING, DIDN'T YOU? THAT'S WHY YOU TOOK SO LONG, RIGHT?
SÍ, MI'JO, BUT THEY WON'T LET CHILDREN IN. YOU'LL SEE HIM WHEN HE COMES HOME.
WHEN IS THAT?
SOON, PROBABLY.

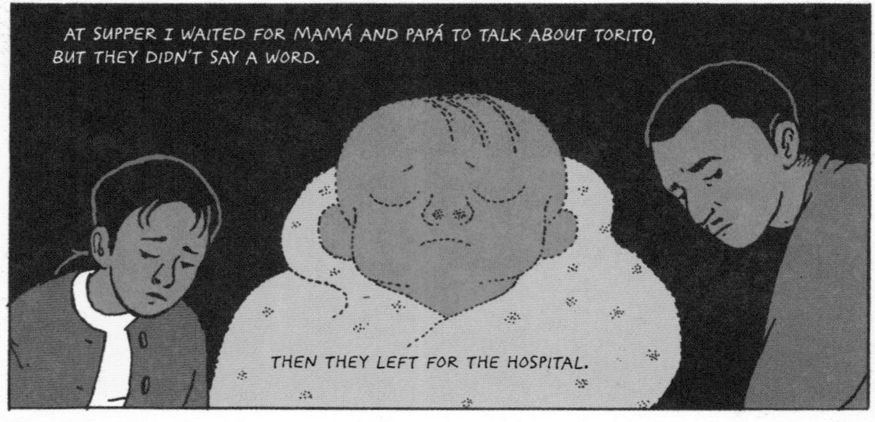
AT SUPPER I WAITED FOR MAMÁ AND PAPÁ TO TALK ABOUT TORITO, BUT THEY DIDN'T SAY A WORD.
THEN THEY LEFT FOR THE HOSPITAL.

TORITO IS A LITTLE BETTER, BUT WE CAN'T BRING HIM HOME UNTIL TOMORROW.

WE HAVE TO PRAY TO THE SANTO NIÑO DE ATOCHA BECAUSE...
...YOUR MAMÁ AND I PROMISED TO PRAY TO HIM EVERY DAY FOR A YEAR IF TORITO GETS WELL.

WE ALL KNELT IN FRONT OF THE SANTO NIÑO. MAMÁ WOULD ALWAYS PRAY TO HIM WHEN ONE OF US GOT SICK.
SHE SAID THE HOLY CHILD JESUS TOOK CARE OF POOR AND SICK PEOPLE, ESPECIALLY CHILDREN.
THE LATE HOUR AND THE REPETITION OF THE PRAYERS MADE ME SLEEPY.

I BEGAN TO DREAM
ABOUT THE SANTO NIÑO DE ATOCHA, WHO SUDDENLY CAME ALIVE,
AND PLACED HIS BASKET AT MY FEET. TINY WHITE BUTTERFLIES EMERGED FROM THE BASKET,

FORMING THEMSELVES
INTO WINGS, LIFTING
ME AND SETTING ME
DOWN NEXT TO TORITO.
THEN TORITO WAS ON THE PRAYER CARD, DRESSED AS THE SAINT.

THE NEXT MORNING, WHEN I TOLD MAMÁ ABOUT MY DREAM, SHE DECIDED TO MAKE TORITO AN OUTFIT.
JUST LIKE THE ONE THE SANTO NIÑO WAS WEARING ON THE CARD.

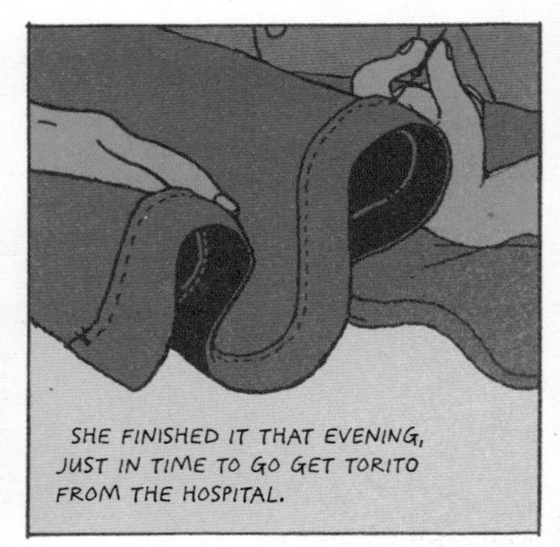
SHE FINISHED IT THAT EVENING, JUST IN TIME TO GO GET TORITO FROM THE HOSPITAL.

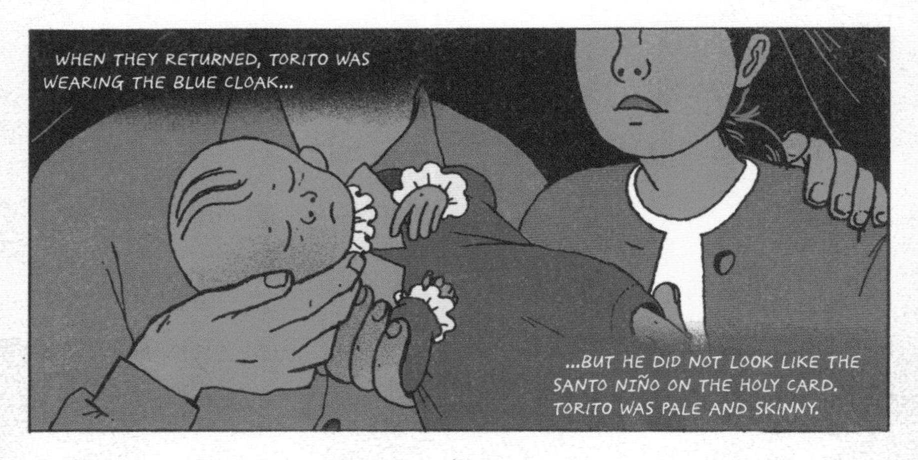
WHEN THEY RETURNED, TORITO WAS WEARING THE BLUE CLOAK...
...BUT HE DID NOT LOOK LIKE THE SANTO NIÑO ON THE HOLY CARD. TORITO WAS PALE AND SKINNY.

MAMÁ, IS TORITO STILL SICK?
YES, MI'JO. THAT'S WHY WE HAVE TO KEEP ON PRAYING.
BUT DIDN'T THE DOCTOR TAKE CARE OF HIM?
REMEMBER, WE HAVE TO KEEP OUR PROMISE. WE WILL PRAY TO THE SANTO NIÑO EVERY DAY, FOR A WHOLE YEAR.

THAT NIGHT, AND EVERY NIGHT FOR AN ENTIRE YEAR...

...WE ALL PRAYED TO THE SANTO NIÑO DE ATOCHA AS WE FOLLOWED THE CROPS FROM PLACE TO PLACE. GRAPES TO COTTON TO STRAWBERRIES AGAIN, WE KEPT PRAYING.

DURING THAT TIME, MAMÁ DRESSED TORITO IN THE BLUE CLOAK AND TOOK IT OFF ONLY WHEN IT NEEDED TO BE WASHED.

ON THE DAY WE COMPLETED THE PROMISE TO THE SANTO NIÑO, WE ALL GATHERED AROUND TORITO.

I HAVE SOMETHING TO TELL YOU.
WHEN WE TOOK TORITO TO THE HOSPITAL...
...THE DOCTOR TOLD US MY SON WOULD DIE. BECAUSE WE HAD WAITED TOO LONG.
HE SAID IT WOULD TAKE A MIRACLE FOR HIM TO LIVE.
I DIDN'T WANT TO BELIEVE HIM.

BUT HE WAS RIGHT.
IT TOOK A MIRACLE.

EL ÁNGEL DE ORO

For
Miguel
Antonio

IT ALWAYS RAINED A LOT IN CORCORAN DURING THE COTTON SEASON...
...BUT THAT YEAR IT RAINED MORE THAN USUAL. AS SOON AS WE ARRIVED FROM FOWLER, WHERE WE HAD PICKED GRAPES, IT STARTED TO POUR.

OUR CABIN WAS ONE OF SEVERAL FARM-WORKER SHACKS, BEHIND WHICH RAN A SMALL CREEK.

THERE WAS NOT A LOT TO DO WHEN IT RAINED.
WE WOULD STAY INDOORS TELLING GHOST STORIES WE HAD HEARD FROM OTHER MIGRANT WORKERS.

WHEN I TIRED OF LISTENING TO THE SAME STORIES, I WATCHED OUR NEIGHBOR'S GOLDFISH.
I SPENT HOURS GLUED TO OUR WINDOW, LOOKING AT THE GOLDFISH GLIDING IN SLOW MOTION.

MAMÁ ENJOYED WATCHING IT TOO. SHE CALLED IT "EL ÁNGEL DE ORO."

PAPÁ SPENT MOST OF HIS TIME WORRYING. WE COULD NOT PICK COTTON WHEN IT WAS WET.
IF THIS RAIN DOESN'T STOP, WE'LL HAVE TO LEAVE AND FIND WORK SOMEWHERE ELSE.

EVEN THE THOUGHT OF RAIN WOULD GIVE PAPÁ A HEADACHE.
LUCKILY FOR ME, I GOT TO GO TO SCHOOL THE FOLLOWING WEEK.
SCHOOL WAS ONLY ABOUT A MILE FROM THE COTTON LABOR CAMP. I COULD SEE THE BUILDING FROM WHERE WE LIVED.

ON MONDAY MORNING, ON THE WAY TO SCHOOL, I MET MIGUELITO, WHO LIVED IN THE SAME LABOR CAMP. HE WAS TWO YEARS OLDER THAN I AND HAD STARTED SCHOOL FOR THE FIRST TIME THAT YEAR A MONTH EARLIER, IN OCTOBER.

HE TOOK ME TO THE MAIN OFFICE AND TRANSLATED INTO SPANISH SOME OF THE QUESTIONS THE PRINCIPAL ASKED ME.

LET'S WALK HOME TOGETHER.
OK!

AFTER SCHOOL, MIGUELITO WAS WAITING FOR ME.

THE PATH HOME WAS MUDDY AND FULL OF PUDDLES, JUST LIKE THE SCHOOL PLAYGROUND. MIGUELITO AND I IMAGINED THE PUDDLES WERE LAKES AND PRETENDED TO BE GIANTS STEPPING OVER THEM. WE COUNTED THE NUMBER OF LAKES WE STEPPED OVER, TRYING TO OUTDO EACH OTHER.
1
2!
3
4!
5
6
7 -AH!

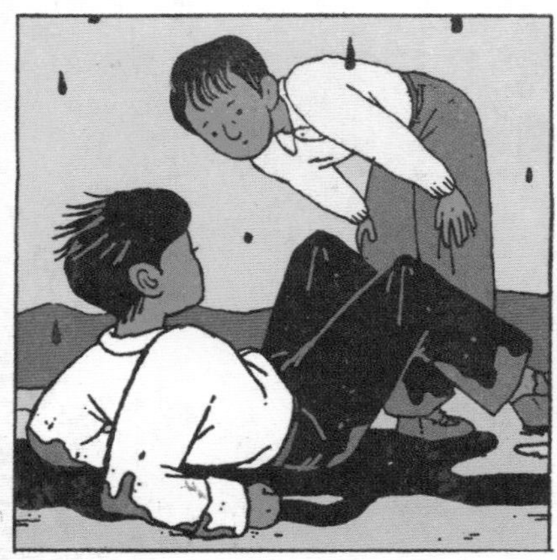

HA HA HA HA HA HA HA HA HA HA HA HA HA HA HA HA HA HA HA HA

WANT TO COME IN?
I HAVE TO GO HOME FIRST. I'LL COME BACK IN A LITTLE WHILE.

I'LL BE IN THE BACK BY THE CREEK. DON'T FORGET, OUR CABIN IS NUMBER 10!

I'M 10 CABINS DOWN FROM YOU: NUMBER 20.

IT WAS COLD AND QUIET INSIDE OUR CABIN.
I WONDER IF HE GETS LONELY.

TOSS
SPLASH

WHAT ARE YOU DOING?

JUST WATCHING THE LITTLE FISH.
DO YOU WANT TO CATCH SOME?
SOME WHAT?
FISH, TONTO!

THESE ARE OUR FISHING POLES.
TOMORROW I'LL BRING THE OTHER STUFF AND WE'LL FINISH MAKING THEM.

THAT NIGHT IT POURED AGAIN, AND IN THE MORNING THE RAIN TURNED TO DRIZZLE.
I HAD HOPED TO MEET MIGUELITO SO WE COULD WALK TO SCHOOL TOGETHER, BUT HE DID NOT SHOW UP.

I DID NOT SEE HIM AT SCHOOL ALL DAY.

WHEN I RETURNED HOME FROM SCHOOL THAT AFTERNOON, I WENT TO SEE IF HE WAS WAITING FOR ME BY THE CREEK.
HE WAS NOT THERE, EITHER.

I HURRIED TO NUMBER 20 AND KNOCKED ON THE DOOR. NO ONE ANSWERED.
20

THE CABIN WAS COMPLETELY EMPTY. MY HEART SANK INTO MY STOMACH.

WHEN I GOT HOME, I STOOD BY OUR WINDOW AND STARED AT OUR NEIGHBOR'S GOLDFISH FOR A LONG TIME.
FINALLY MY FAMILY RETURNED. THEY HAD SPENT ALL DAY DRIVING AROUND, LOOKING FOR WORK.

IT RAINED SO MUCH
THAT NIGHT THAT THE
CREEK FLOODED INTO
THE DIRT STREETS...

WHEN THE SUN FINALLY
EMERGED, THE LAKE SPLIT INTO
HUNDREDS OF SMALL PUDDLES
THROUGHOUT THE LABOR CAMP.

I DISCOVERED
LITTLE GRAY FISH
IN THE PUDDLES.
HOW DID THEY GET
THERE?

IN THE SMALLER PUDDLES THE FISH WERE DYING.
THE MUD WAS SUFFOCATING THEM.

AS I GAZED AT THE DEAD FISH, THE IMAGE OF THE
NEIGHBOR'S GOLDFISH FLASHED IN MY MIND.

AFTER A COUPLE HOURS OF TAKING THE DYING FISH TO THE CREEK, I WAS EXHAUSTED. THERE WERE TOO MANY. I COULD NOT WORK FAST ENOUGH TO SAVE THEM ALL.
I PRAYED FOR THEM BUT THE SUN KEPT BEATING DOWN.

I PICKED UP ONE LAST SMALL, DYING FISH AND TOOK IT TO OUR NEXT-DOOR NEIGHBOR.
KNOCK
KNOCK
KNOCK

KNOCK
KNOCK

THE LITTLE GRAY FISH LOOKED UP AT ME, OPENING AND CLOSING ITS MOUTH.

HILLS BROS
COFFEE

THAT EVENING I LOOKED THROUGH THE
WINDOW INTO OUR NEIGHBOR'S CABIN.

THE NEXT MORNING I TOOK THE FISHING ROD MIGUELITO HAD GIVEN ME, PLACED IT GENTLY IN THE CREEK...
...AND WATCHED IT FLOAT AWAY.

Christmas Gift

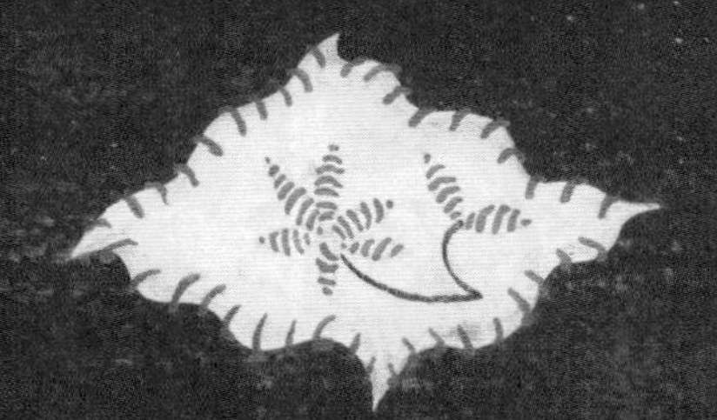

A LITTLE WHILE BEFORE CHRISTMAS, PAPÁ DECIDED WE SHOULD MOVE FROM CORCORAN AND LOOK FOR WORK ELSEWHERE.

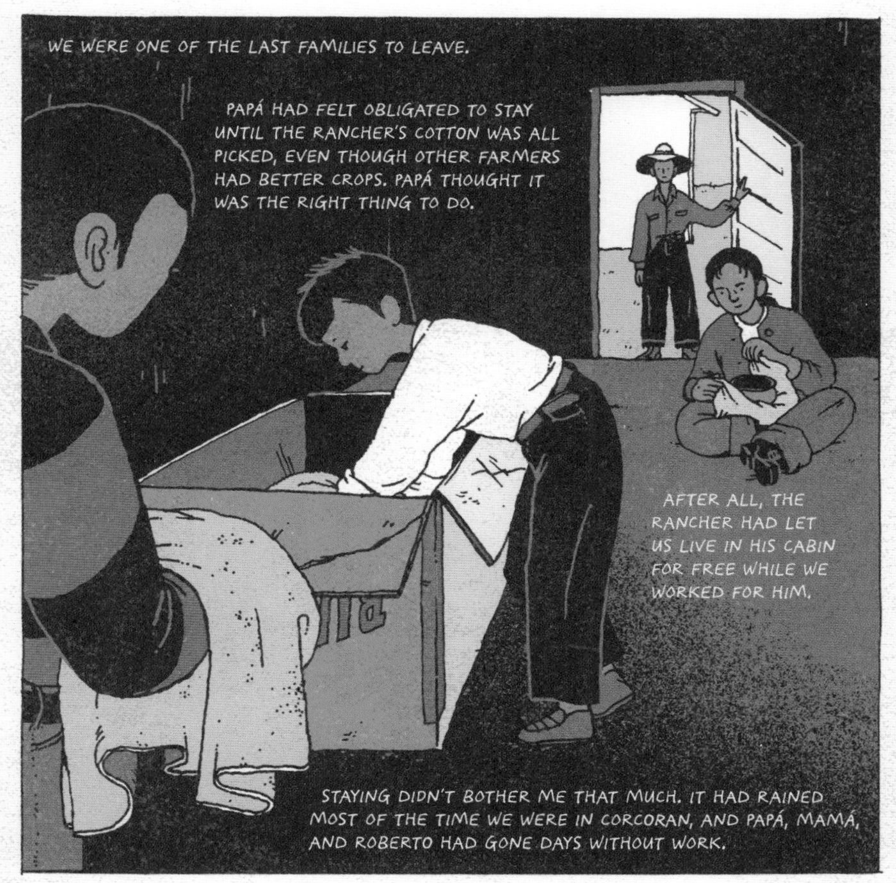
WE WERE ONE OF THE LAST FAMILIES TO LEAVE.
PAPÁ HAD FELT OBLIGATED TO STAY UNTIL THE RANCHER'S COTTON WAS ALL PICKED, EVEN THOUGH OTHER FARMERS HAD BETTER CROPS. PAPÁ THOUGHT IT WAS THE RIGHT THING TO DO.
AFTER ALL, THE RANCHER HAD LET US LIVE IN HIS CABIN FOR FREE WHILE WE WORKED FOR HIM.
STAYING DIDN'T BOTHER ME THAT MUCH. IT HAD RAINED MOST OF THE TIME WE WERE IN CORCORAN, AND PAPÁ, MAMÁ, AND ROBERTO HAD GONE DAYS WITHOUT WORK.

SOMETIMES WE WENT INTO TOWN IN OUR CARCACHITA TO LOOK FOR FOOD IN THE TRASH BEHIND GROCERY STORES.
WE PICKED UP PARTLY SPOILED FRUITS AND VEGETABLES. MAMÁ SLICED OFF THE ROTTEN PARTS AND MADE SOUP.

SHE MIXED THE VEGETABLES WITH BONES SHE BOUGHT AT THE BUTCHER SHOP.
SHE TOLD THE BUTCHER THE BONES WERE FOR A DOG. THE BUTCHER MUST HAVE KNOWN THE BONES WERE FOR US...
...BECAUSE HE LEFT MORE AND MORE PIECES OF MEAT ON THEM EACH TIME MAMÁ WENT BACK.

AS WE WERE PACKING TO LEAVE CORCORAN THAT DECEMBER...
KNOCK
KNOCK

SORRY TO BOTHER YOU, BUT YOU KNOW, WITH ALL THIS RAIN, AND MY WIFE EXPECTING...

WELL, WE THOUGHT...YOU COULD HELP US OUT A BIT...
PERHAPS YOU COULD GIVE US 50 CENTS FOR THIS?
LOOK, IT'S PURE LEATHER.
ALMOST BRAND-NEW.

I AM SORRY.
I WISH I COULD, PAISANO, BUT WE'RE BROKE TOO.
25 CENTS?
HOW ABOUT 10 CENTS FOR THIS HANDKERCHIEF? MY WIFE DID THE NEEDLEWORK ON IT.
IT'S BEAUTIFUL. QUE DIOS LOS BENDIGA.
I AM VERY SORRY.

WHEN I HEARD HIM SAY, "WE'RE BROKE TOO," I PANICKED.
IT CAN'T BE LIKE LAST YEAR.

SOON WE WERE HEADING NORTH.

WE WERE LEAVING ONLY THREE WEEKS AFTER I HAD ENROLLED IN FOURTH GRADE.

AS WE DROVE BY THE SCHOOL, I SAW SOME KIDS I KNEW ON THE PLAYGROUND.
I IMAGINED MYSELF PLAYING WITH THEM WITH THE BALL I WOULD GET FOR CHRISTMAS.
I WAVED TO THEM, BUT THEY DID NOT SEE ME.

AFTER STOPPING AT SEVERAL PLACES, WE FOUND A RANCHER IN VISALIA WHO STILL HAD A FEW COTTON FIELDS TO BE PICKED. HE OFFERED US WORK AND A TENT TO LIVE IN.

WE PLACED SOME CARDBOARD ON THE DIRT FLOOR, THEN LAID OUR WIDE MATTRESS ON IT.

ALL OF US—PAPÁ, MAMÁ, ROBERTO, TRAMPITA, TORITO, RUBÉN, MY BABY BROTHER, AND I—SLEPT ON THE MATTRESS TO KEEP WARM.

AS CHRISTMAS DREW CLOSER, THE MORE ANXIOUS AND EXCITED I BECAME, AND WHEN DECEMBER 24 FINALLY ARRIVED, TIME SEEMED TO STAND STILL.
ONE MORE DAY TO WAIT.
THAT EVENING, AFTER SUPPER, MAMÁ TOLD US THE STORY OF THE BIRTH OF JESUS AND THE THREE WISE MEN WHO BROUGHT HIM GIFTS.
I ONLY HALF LISTENED, WANTING THE EVENING TO END QUICKLY AND MORNING TO COME.

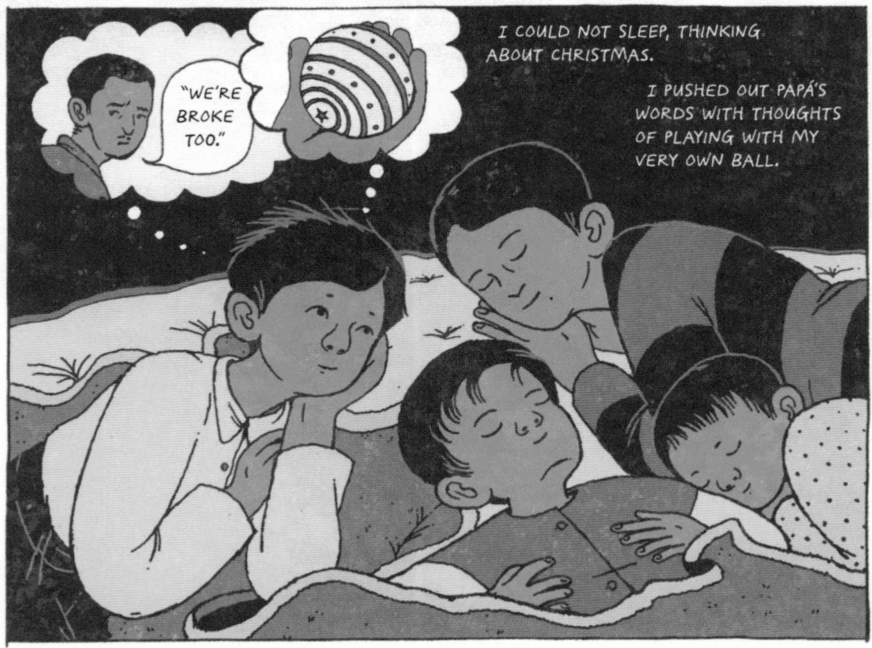
"WE'RE BROKE TOO."
I COULD NOT SLEEP, THINKING ABOUT CHRISTMAS.
I PUSHED OUT PAPÁ'S WORDS WITH THOUGHTS OF PLAYING WITH MY VERY OWN BALL.

THINKING WE WERE ALL ASLEEP, MAMÁ WRAPPED PRESENTS BY THE LIGHT OF THE KEROSENE LAMP.

I TRIED TO SEE WHAT GIFTS SHE WAS WRAPPING.
BUT I COULD SEE ONLY HER WEATHERWORN FACE.
SILENT TEARS RAN DOWN HER CHEEKS.
I DID NOT KNOW WHY.

AT DAWN, MY BROTHERS AND I SCRAMBLED TO GET THE PRESENTS.

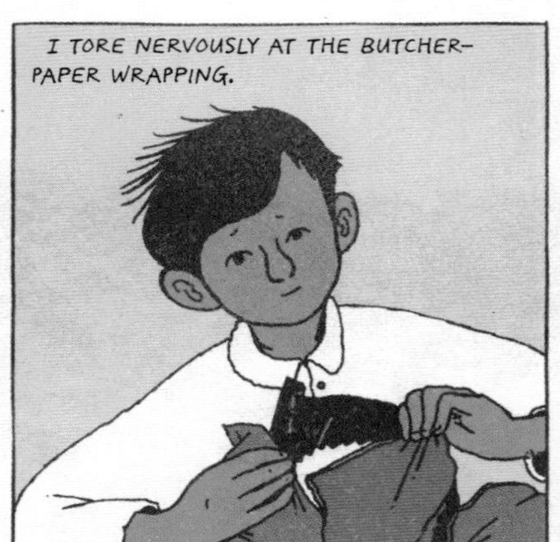
I TORE NERVOUSLY AT THE BUTCHER-PAPER WRAPPING.

A BAG OF CANDY FOR EACH OF US.

WE LOOKED SADLY AT ONE ANOTHER.

SEARCHING FOR WORDS TO TELL MAMÁ HOW I FELT, I LOOKED UP AT HER AND SAW HER EYES WERE FULL OF TEARS. THEN FROM UNDER THE MATTRESS, PAPA PULLED OUT THE EMBROIDERED HANDKERCHIEF.
LIFT
TUG

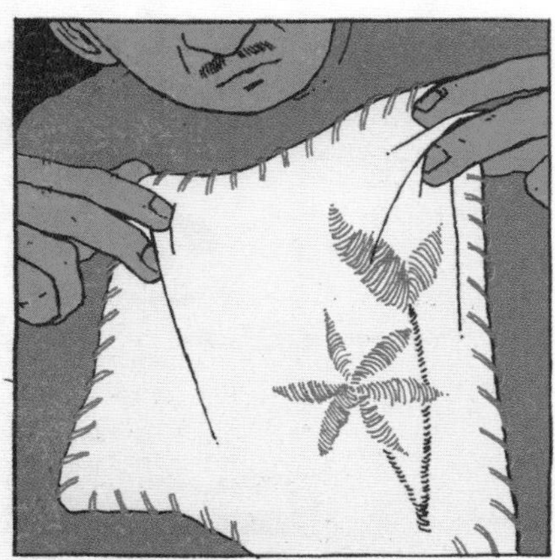

FELIZ NAVIDAD, VIEJA.

DEATH FORGIVEN

EL PERICO, MY CLOSE FRIEND, WAS A RED, GREEN, AND YELLOW PARROT THAT HAD BEEN SMUGGLED FROM MEXICO BY DON PANCHO, AN UNDOCUMENTED FARM WORKER WHO WAS MY FATHER'S FRIEND.
WHEN WE FIRST GOT EL PERICO, HE SPENT MOST OF HIS TIME IN A CAGE ROBERTO HAD BUILT. BUT ONCE HE LEARNED TO TRUST US, HE WANDERED AROUND THE DILAPIDATED GARAGE WHERE WE LIVED WHILE HARVESTING MR. JACOBSON'S VINEYARDS IN FRESNO.
¡PERIQUITO BONITO!
¡PERIQUITO BONITO! ¡PERIQUITO BONITO!
HIS FAVORITE PASTIME WAS WALKING BACK AND FORTH ACROSS A WIRE THAT MAMÁ USED TO HANG OUR CLOTHES TO DRY.
¡PERIQUITO BONITO!
KISS
HE WOULD GRAB MY FINGER. I WOULD LIFT HIM AND BRING HIM CLOSE TO MY FACE, TOUCHING MY NOSE TO HIS BEAK UNTIL I WOULD KISS HIS HEAD.

THE AFFECTION EL PERICO AND I HAD FOR EACH OTHER WAS MATCHED ONLY BY HIS ATTACHMENT TO CATARINA...
...A CAT THAT BELONGED TO CHICO AND PILAR, WHO, LIKE THE PARROT, WERE UNDOCUMENTED.

THEY LIVED IN ONE OF THE STABLES NEXT TO OUR GARAGE.

CHICO, PILAR, AND CATARINA WOULD VISIT US OFTEN IN THE EVENINGS AFTER WORK. EL PERICO AND CATARINA GREW ON EACH OTHER LITTLE BY LITTLE.
¡PERIQUITO BONITO!
EVENTUALLY, THEY BECAME SUCH GOOD FRIENDS THAT THEY WOULD EVEN EAT LEFTOVERS—BEANS, RICE, AND POTATOES—FROM THE SAME PLATE.

WHEN CHICO AND PILAR VISITED WITHOUT CATARINA, EL PERICO WOULD GET VERY UPSET.
THIS WOULD IRRITATE MY FATHER, WHO COULD NOT STAND ANY NOISE...
...ESPECIALLY WHEN HE WAS TIRED FROM WORK, WHICH WAS MOST OF THE TIME.

ONE EARLY EVENING, CHICO AND PILAR CAME BY THEMSELVES, WITHOUT CATARINA.
SQUAWK?

SQUAWK! SQUAWK!
THE NOISE STRUCK MY FATHER LIKE LIGHTNING.
SQUAWK! SQUAWK!
SQUAWK!
SQUAWK!
HE HAD BEEN IN A TERRIBLE MOOD THE PAST FEW DAYS...
HE WAS NOT SURE WHERE WE WOULD WORK, NOW THAT THE GRAPE SEASON WAS ALMOST OVER.
SQUAWK!
SQUAWK!

SQUAWK!
SQUAWK!
SQUAWK!
SQUAW
WWW
WWWWK!

AAAAAH
AAAAAA
AAH

I FELT AS THOUGH SOMEONE HAD RIPPED MY HEART OUT. I THREW THE GARAGE DOOR OPEN AND RAN AS FAST AS I COULD.

EVEN FROM A STORAGE SHED A HALF MILE AWAY, THE SHOUTING, SCREAMING, AND CRYING FROM OUR HOUSE CHASED ME.

SANTA MARÍA, MADRE DE DIOS, RUEGA SEÑORA POR NOSOTROS LOS PECADORES AHORA Y EN LA HORA DE NUESTRA MUERTE, AMÉN.
THE REPETITION OF THE PRAYER SLOWLY COMFORTED AND SOOTHED MY SOUL.
THEN I PRAYED FOR MY FATHER.

THE NEXT DAY, WE DUG A HOLE A FOOT DEEP BEHIND THE GARAGE.

I VISITED EL PERICO'S GRAVE EVERY DAY UNTIL WE MOVED AGAIN.

COTTON SACK

IN LATE OCTOBER, AFTER THE GRAPE SEASON WAS OVER, WE LEFT MR. JACOBSON'S VINEYARDS IN FRESNO AND HEADED FOR CORCORAN.
WE PASSED VINEYARD AFTER VINEYARD. STRIPPED OF THEIR GRAPES, THE VINES WERE NOW DRAPED IN YELLOW, ORANGE, AND BROWN LEAVES.
WITHIN A COUPLE OF HOURS, THE VINEYARDS GAVE WAY TO COTTON FIELDS.

AFTER STOPPING AT THREE LABOR CAMPS, WE FOUND ONE THAT WOULD GIVE US WORK AND A ONE-ROOM CABIN TO LIVE IN.

AFTER SUPPER THAT FIRST NIGHT, PAPÁ UNFOLDED THE COTTON SACKS AND LAID THEM OUT ON THE FLOOR FOR THE NEXT DAY.

WHERE IS MINE? DON'T I GET ONE? LAST YEAR I PICKED WITHOUT A SACK!
YOU'RE STILL TOO LITTLE TO HAVE YOUR OWN, PANCHITO.

STRETCH THIS FOR ME.

AFTER THE LAST STITCH, PAPÁ TIED THE SACK TO HIS WAIST.
HE LOOKED LIKE A KANGAROO.

WHEN HE FINISHED SEWING MAMÁ'S SACK, SHE TRIED IT ON TOO.

HA!

WHAT'S SO FUNNY?
THIS IS THE PRETTIEST WEDDING DRESS I'VE EVER SEEN!

WHEN IT WAS TIME FOR BED, PAPÁ FOLDED HIS COTTON SACK TO USE AS A PILLOW.

HE PLACED A GLASS OF WATER ON THE FLOOR NEAR THE BED WITH
BAYER
HIS ASPIRINS,
CAMEL
HIS CIGARETTES,
AND AN EMPTY COFFEE CAN...
Folger's
...WHICH WE WOULD ALL USE DURING THE NIGHT WHEN IT WAS TOO COLD TO GO TO THE OUTHOUSE.

ROBERTO, TRAMPITA, TORITO, AND I KNELT IN FRONT OF THE VIRGEN DE GUADALUPE AND SAID OUR PRAYERS SILENTLY.

MAMÁ WRAPPED RORRA, MY NEWBORN SISTER, IN A BLANKET, LAID HER IN A CRATE, AND KISSED HER GOOD NIGHT.

WE SNUGGLED AGAINST ONE ANOTHER TO KEEP WARM.
MY PARENTS HAD AN ADVANTAGE OVER US BECAUSE OUR LEGS DID NOT REACH THE OTHER END OF THE MATTRESS.
THEIR FEET, HOWEVER, DID, AND SOMETIMES I WOULD WAKE UP FACING MAMÁ'S AND PAPÁ'S TOES.

THE POUNDING OF RAIN ON THE ROOF WOKE ME SEVERAL TIMES THAT FIRST NIGHT. EVERY TIME I OPENED MY EYES, I WOULD SEE THE TIP OF PAPÁ'S CIGARETTE GLOWING IN THE DARK. OTHER TIMES I HEARD THE RATTLE OF HIS ASPIRIN BOTTLE.
I DID NOT MIND THE RAIN BECAUSE IT MEANT I COULD SLEEP IN THE NEXT MORNING. THE COTTON WOULD BE TOO WET TO PICK. WE GOT PAID THREE CENTS A POUND. MOST RANCHERS DID NOT LET US PICK WET COTTON BECAUSE IT WEIGHED MORE THAN WHEN IT WAS DRY.

THE NEXT MORNING, PAPÁ CURSED THE RAIN.

MAMÁ USED A LEAD PIPE TO ROLL DOUGH ON A BOARD ATOP THE BOXES THAT SERVED AS OUR DINING TABLE.

SHE THEN COOKED THE TORTILLAS ON A COMAL ON OUR SMALL KEROSENE STOVE.
SHE USUALLY COOKED A POT OF BEANS ON THE OTHER BURNER.

PAPÁ DROVE IN OUR CARCACHITA TO THE NEAREST GAS STATION TO FILL A ONE-GALLON BOTTLE WITH DRINKING WATER AND TO GET MORE KEROSENE FOR THE STOVE. MAMÁ TOLD US TO BE VERY QUIET BECAUSE PAPÁ WAS NOT FEELING WELL THAT DAY.
REMEMBER, HE DOES NOT LIKE NOISE.

ON THIS FIRST DAY OF PICKING AFTER THE RAIN, WE AND A CARAVAN OF OLD BATTERED CARS AND TRUCKS FOLLOWED THE CONTRATISTA.

AFTER ABOUT FIVE MILES, THE CONTRATISTA PULLED OVER AND POINTED TO A COTTON FIELD.
IT STRETCHED AS FAR AS THE EYE COULD SEE.

REMEMBER, COTTON BOLLS ARE LIKE ROSES. THEY ARE PRETTY, BUT THEY CAN HURT YOU.
SÍ, PAPÁ. I REMEMBER THE SHELL IS LIKE A CAT'S CLAW.

ALL THE PICKERS BUT ME HAD THEIR OWN SACKS AND THEIR OWN ROW.
I PICKED COTTON FROM MAMÁ'S ROW AND PILED IT ON THE GROUND. I THEN MOVED TO PAPÁ'S ROW AND DID THE SAME.
ROBERTO DID NOT NEED MY HELP.

WHEN MAMÁ'S SACK WAS TOO HEAVY TO DRAG, ROBERTO AND I TOOK IT TO THE WEIGH STATION, A QUARTER OF A MILE AHEAD.

YOU'RE REALLY STRONG FOR SUCH A LITTLE GUY. HOW OLD ARE YOU?
FOURTEEN, ALMOST FIFTEEN.

NO FOOLING! AND WHERE IS YOUR SACK, MOCOSO?
I PRETENDED NOT TO HEAR HIM.
PAPÁ CARRIED HIS OWN SACK, BUT ROBERTO EMPTIED IT ONTO A TRAILER BECAUSE OF PAPÁ'S BAD BACK.

AT THE END OF THE DAY, THE CONTRATISTA HANDED MY FATHER EIGHTEEN DOLLARS.
NOT BAD! SIX HUNDRED POUNDS!
WE COULD HAVE DONE BETTER IF I HAD HAD MY OWN SACK.

BY THE MIDDLE OF NOVEMBER, THE COTTON FIELDS HAD BEEN PICKED.
THE CONTRATISTA INFORMED PAPÁ THAT WE COULD STAY IN THE CABIN UNTIL THE END OF THE SECOND PICKING, OR LA BOLA.
LA BOLA, WHICH STARTED IN TWO WEEKS, WAS MESSY AND DIRTY.
IT INVOLVED HARVESTING EVERYTHING LEFT ON THE PLANTS, INCLUDING COTTON SHELLS AND LEAVES.

FOR THE NEXT FEW DAYS, PAPÁ, MAMÁ, AND ROBERTO WOULD LEAVE THE CABIN EARLY EACH MORNING TO LOOK FOR WORK, TAKING TORITO, RUBÉN, AND RORRA WITH THEM.
TRAMPITA AND I WENT TO SCHOOL AND JOINED THEM ON WEEKENDS TO LOOK FOR WORK.

AT DAWN ON THANKSGIVING, PAPÁ, ROBERTO, AND I DROVE FOR MILES, LOOKING FOR FIELDS THAT WERE STILL BEING PICKED.
DURING THAT FOUR-DAY WEEKEND, I WAS DETERMINED TO PROVE TO PAPÁ THAT I SHOULD GET MY OWN SACK.

¡ALLÁ!

YOU CAN START ANYTIME YOU WANT, BUT YOU MIGHT WANT TO WAIT UNTIL IT GETS WARMER. YOU CAN JOIN THE OTHERS AROUND THE FIRE.

YOU CAN WAIT, BUT I AM GOING TO PICK.

I WOULD PROVE TO PAPÁ THAT I WAS GROWN-UP ENOUGH FOR MY OWN COTTON SACK.
I FOLLOWED HIM AND ROBERTO INTO THE FIELD.

WITHIN SECONDS MY TOES WERE NUMB.
I COULD HARDLY MOVE MY FINGERS. MY
HANDS TURNED RED AND PURPLE.

ZIIIIIP

PPSSSSSSSS

INSTANTLY, I FELT FIRE AS THE SALT STUNG THE SCRATCHES ON MY SKIN.
THEN, AS THE LIQUID QUICKLY COOLED, MY HANDS FELT LIKE ICE.

I COULD NOT GO ON.

GO OVER TO THE FIRE.

I KNEW THEN I HAD NOT YET EARNED MY OWN COTTON SACK.

THE CIRCUIT

IT WAS THAT TIME OF YEAR AGAIN.
THE PEAK OF THE STRAWBERRY SEASON WAS OVER IN SANTA MARIA.
AS THE LAST DAYS OF AUGUST DISAPPEARED, SO DID THE NUMBER OF BRACEROS. BY SUNDAY, ONLY ONE BRACERO—THE BEST PICKER—CAME TO WORK.
I LIKED HIM. HE WAS FROM JALISCO, THE SAME STATE IN MEXICO MY FAMILY WAS FROM. THAT SUNDAY WAS THE LAST TIME I SAW HIM.
WHEN THE SUN HAD SUNK BELOW THE MOUNTAINS, ITO SIGNALED TO US.
YA ES HORA. TIME TO GO HOME!
THOSE WERE THE WORDS I WOULD WAIT FOR TWELVE HOURS A DAY, EVERY DAY, SEVEN DAYS A WEEK.

WHEN I OPENED THE FRONT DOOR TO THE SHACK, I STOPPED.
I SUDDENLY FELT THE WEIGHT OF HOURS, DAYS, WEEKS, AND MONTHS OF WORK.
KNOWING WHAT WAS IN STORE FOR ME IN FRESNO BROUGHT TEARS TO MY EYES.

THAT NIGHT I COULD NOT SLEEP. I LAY IN BED THINKING ABOUT HOW MUCH I HATED MOVING AGAIN.

A LITTLE BEFORE FIVE, PAPÁ WOKE EVERYONE UP.
THE YELLING AND SCREAMING OF MY LITTLE BROTHERS AND SISTER, FOR WHOM MOVING WAS A GREAT ADVENTURE, BROKE THE SILENCE OF DAWN.

PAPÁ WAS VERY PROUD OF HIS JALOPY.
HE HAD A RIGHT TO BE.

HE HAD EXAMINED
EVERY INCH BEFORE
BUYING IT.

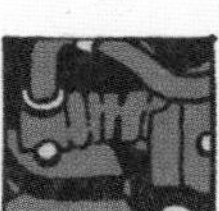

AS WE DROVE AWAY, I LOOKED AT OUR LITTLE SHACK FOR THE LAST TIME.

AT SUNSET WE REACHED A LABOR CAMP NEAR FRESNO.

SINCE PAPÁ DID NOT SPEAK ENGLISH, MAMÁ ASKED THE CAMP FOREMAN IF HE NEEDED ANY MORE WORKERS.
WE DON'T NEED NO MORE. CHECK WITH SULLIVAN DOWN THE ROAD. CAN'T MISS HIM. HE LIVES IN A BIG WHITE HOUSE WITH A FENCE AROUND IT.

DING DONG

SWING

WE HAVE WORK!

MR. SULLIVAN SAID WE CAN STAY THERE THE WHOLE SEASON.

THE WINDOWLESS GARAGE WAS WORN OUT BY THE YEARS.

THE WALLS, EATEN BY TERMITES, STRAINED TO SUPPORT THE ROOF FULL OF HOLES.
THE DIRT FLOOR, POPULATED BY EARTHWORMS, LOOKED LIKE A GRAY ROAD MAP.

THAT NIGHT, BY THE LIGHT OF A KEROSENE LAMP, WE UNPACKED AND CLEANED OUR NEW HOME.

WE PLUGGED THE HOLES WITH OLD NEWSPAPERS.

YOU AND THE LITTLE ONES SLEEP ON THE MATTRESS.
ROBERTO, PANCHITO, AND I WILL SLEEP OUTSIDE UNDER THE TREES.

EARLY THE NEXT MORNING, MR. SULLIVAN SHOWED US WHERE HIS CROP WAS.

AFTER BREAKFAST, PAPÁ, ROBERTO, AND I HEADED FOR THE VINEYARD TO PICK.

AROUND NINE O'CLOCK, THE TEMPERATURE HAD RISEN TO ALMOST 100 DEGREES.
I WAS COMPLETELY SOAKED IN SWEAT, AND MY MOUTH FELT AS IF I HAD BEEN CHEWING ON A HANDKERCHIEF.

DON'T DRINK TOO MUCH; YOU'LL GET SICK.

NO SOONER HAD HE SAID THAT THAN I FELT SICK TO MY STOMACH.

ALL I COULD HEAR WAS THE DRONE OF INSECTS.

SLOWLY I BEGAN TO RECOVER.

BUT I STILL FELT DIZZY WHEN WE BROKE FOR LUNCH AFTER TWO O'CLOCK.

HERE COMES THE SCHOOL BUS!

TIENEN QUE TENER CUIDADO.
ROBERTO AND I HID. AS THE NEATLY DRESSED BOYS GOT OFF, THEY CROSSED THE STREET, AND THE BUS DROVE AWAY.

AFTER LUNCH, THE BUZZING INSECTS, OUR WET SWEAT, AND THE HOT, DRY DUST MADE THE AFTERNOON SEEM TO LAST FOREVER.
FINALLY, THE MOUNTAINS AROUND THE VALLEY REACHED OUT AND SWALLOWED THE SUN.

WITHIN AN HOUR IT WAS TOO DARK TO CONTINUE PICKING.
VÁMONOS.
PAPÁ BEGAN TO FIGURE OUT HOW MUCH WE HAD EARNED OUR FIRST DAY.
QUINCE.

MAMÁ HAD COOKED A SPECIAL MEAL FOR US OF RICE AND TORTILLAS WITH CARNE CON CHILE, MY FAVORITE DISH.

THE NEXT MORNING, I COULD HARDLY MOVE. MY BODY ACHED ALL OVER. I FELT LITTLE CONTROL OVER MY ARMS AND LEGS.
THIS FEELING WENT ON EVERY MORNING FOR DAYS UNTIL MY MUSCLES FINALLY GOT USED TO THE WORK.

BY THE FIRST WEEK OF NOVEMBER, THE GRAPE SEASON WAS OVER AND I COULD GO TO SCHOOL.
I WOKE UP, LOOKED AT THE STARS, AND SAVORED THE THOUGHT OF NOT GOING TO WORK.

AT BREAKFAST, I DIDN'T WANT TO FACE ROBERTO.
HE WOULD NOT GO TO SCHOOL UNTIL THE COTTON SEASON WAS OVER IN FEBRUARY.

PRINCIPAL
KNOCK KNOCK
MAY I HELP YOU?
I HAD NOT HEARD ENGLISH FOR MONTHS. FOR A FEW SECONDS I REMAINED SPEECHLESS.
UM...I WANT TO ENROLL IN THE SIXTH GRADE.

THIS IS MR. LEMA. HE'LL BE YOUR TEACHER.

WHEN EVERYONE'S EYES FELL ON ME...
...I WISHED I WERE WITH PAPÁ AND ROBERTO PICKING COTTON.

THE FIRST THING WE HAVE TO DO IS FINISH READING THE STORY WE BEGAN YESTERDAY.
WE ARE ON PAGE 125.

WOULD YOU LIKE TO READ?

YOU CAN READ LATER.

DURING RECESS, I WENT INTO THE RESTROOM AND OPENED MY ENGLISH BOOK TO PAGE 125.

I BEGAN TO READ IN A LOW VOICE, PRETENDING I WAS IN CLASS.
THERE WERE MANY WORDS I DID NOT KNOW:
pitch
trance
abyss
hearthstone
rendezvous
undaunted

COULD YOU HELP ME WITH THE NEW WORDS?
GLADLY.

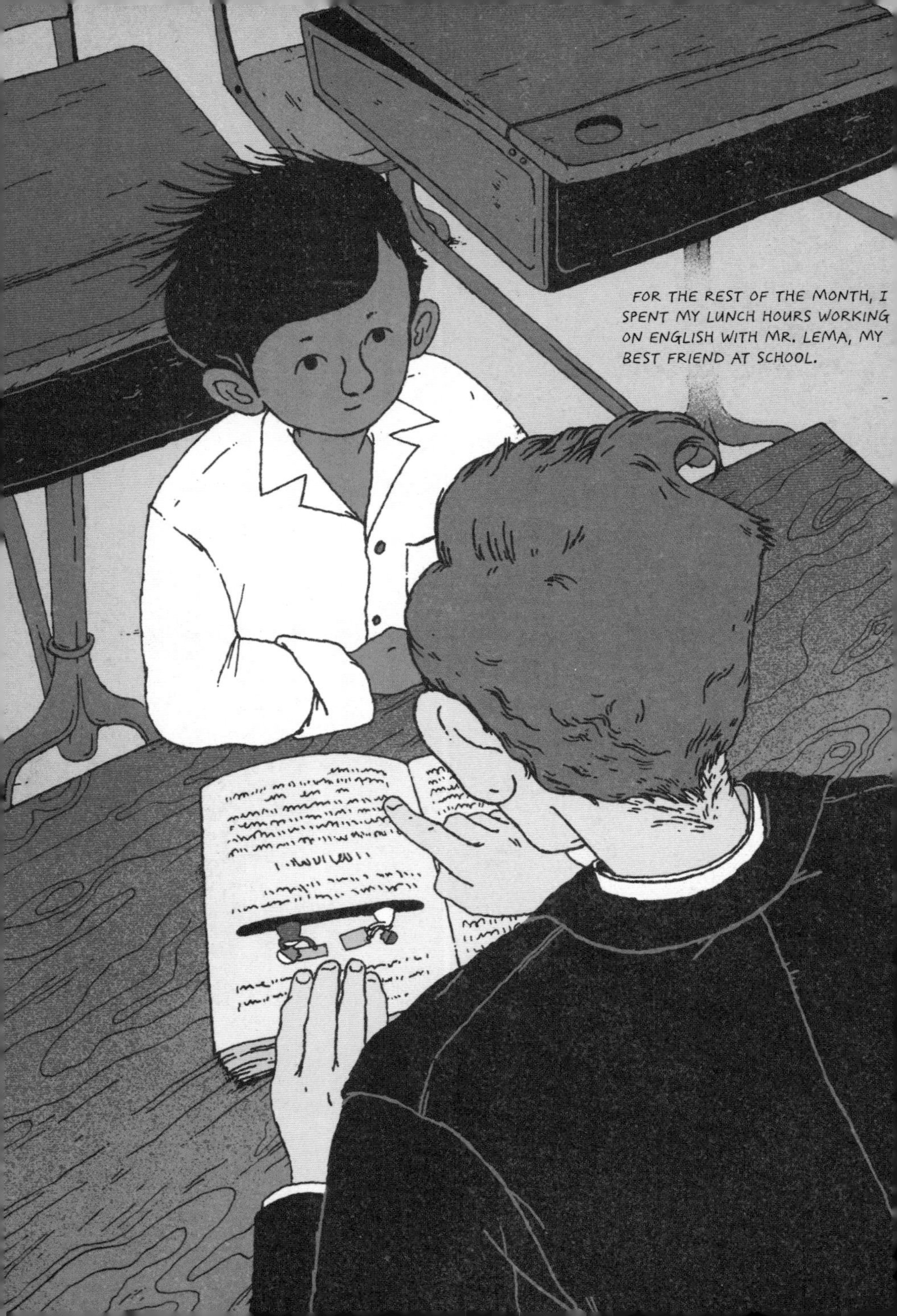
FOR THE REST OF THE MONTH, I SPENT MY LUNCH HOURS WORKING ON ENGLISH WITH MR. LEMA, MY BEST FRIEND AT SCHOOL.

ONE FRIDAY DURING LUNCH HOUR, MR. LEMA TOOK ME TO THE MUSIC ROOM.
DO YOU LIKE MUSIC?

YES...I LIKE CORRIDOS.

THE SOUND GAVE ME GOOSE BUMPS. I KNEW THAT SOUND. I HAD HEARD IT IN MANY CORRIDOS.

HOW WOULD YOU LIKE TO LEARN HOW TO PLAY IT?
I'LL TEACH YOU DURING OUR LUNCH HOURS.

THAT DAY I COULD HARDLY WAIT TO TELL PAPÁ AND MAMÁ THE GREAT NEWS.

I THOUGHT MY LITTLE BROTHERS AND SISTER WERE JUST HAPPY TO SEE ME.

UNTIL I OPENED THE DOOR TO OUR HOME...

...AND SAW THAT EVERYTHING WE OWNED WAS
PACKED IN CARDBOARD BOXES.

LEARNING the GAME

I WAS IN A BAD MOOD. IT WAS THE LAST DAY OF SEVENTH GRADE BEFORE SUMMER VACATION. WHILE CLASSMATES WERE EXCITED ABOUT GOING AWAY TO SUMMER CAMP OR ON SUMMER TRIPS, I HAD BEEN TRYING NOT TO THINK ABOUT THE LAST DAY AT SCHOOL.

ON THE BUS, I BEGAN FIGURING OUT HOW LONG I HAD UNTIL SCHOOL WOULD START AGAIN FOR ME: ON THE SECOND WEEK OF NOVEMBER.
TEN WEEKS PICKING STRAWBERRIES IN SANTA MARIA. ANOTHER EIGHT HARVESTING GRAPES IN FRESNO AND ONE WEEK PICKING COTTON IN CORCORAN.
I STARTED TO GET A HEADACHE.
132 MORE DAYS AFTER TODAY.

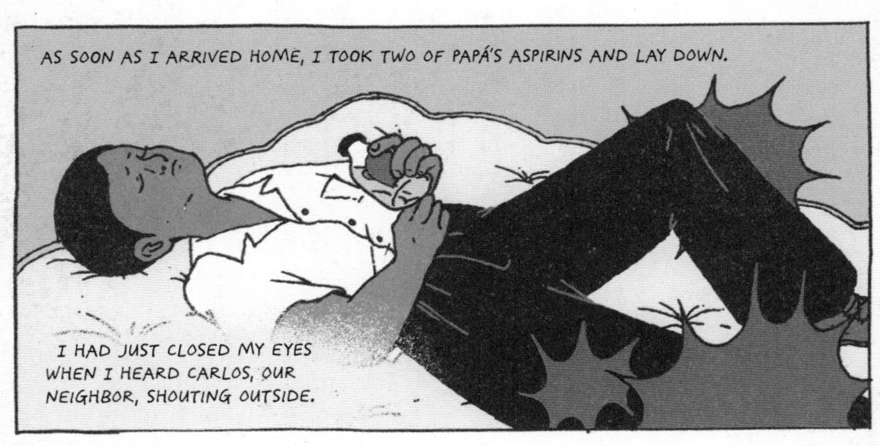
AS SOON AS I ARRIVED HOME, I TOOK TWO OF PAPÁ'S ASPIRINS AND LAY DOWN.
I HAD JUST CLOSED MY EYES WHEN I HEARD CARLOS, OUR NEIGHBOR, SHOUTING OUTSIDE.

THE GAME WAS KICK-THE-CAN.
I PLAYED IT WITH CARLOS AND MY YOUNGER BROTHERS ON SCHOOL DAYS WHEN I HAD NO HOMEWORK...
COME ON, PANCHITO, WE'RE STARTING THE GAME!
...AND ON WEEKENDS WHEN I WAS NOT TOO TIRED FROM WORKING IN THE FIELDS.

I LIKED THE GAME, BUT I DID NOT ENJOY PLAYING WITH CARLOS.
HURRY, OR ELSE! YOU'RE MAKING US WAIT!
HE WAS OLDER AND OFTEN REMINDED ME OF IT, ESPECIALLY WHEN I DISAGREED WITH HIM.
IF WE WANTED TO PLAY, WE HAD TO FOLLOW HIS RULES.

THE MORE WE PLAYED, THE LESS I THOUGHT ABOUT MY TROUBLES. EVEN MY HEADACHE WENT AWAY.

RING RING RING

THE NEXT MORNING, WHEN I SAW ROBERTO PUTTING ON HIS WORK CLOTHES, I REMEMBERED WE WERE GOING TO THE FIELDS, NOT SCHOOL.
TIME TO GET UP!

ITO WAS WAITING FOR US WHEN WE ARRIVED. THEN A PICKUP TRUCK SHOWED UP, AND THE DRIVER ORDERED HIS PASSENGER IN BACK TO GET OUT.

WHO'S THAT?
DON'T POINT. IT'S BAD MANNERS. HE'S MR. DÍAZ, THE CONTRATISTA.
HE RUNS THE BRACERO CAMP FOR SHEEHEY STRAWBERRY FARMS. THE MAN WITH HIM IS ONE OF THE BRACEROS.

THIS IS GABRIEL.

¡HOLA!
¡HOLA!

THIS IS MY FIRST TIME HARVESTING STRAWBERRIES. WILL YOU SHOW ME HOW TO PICK?
IT'S EASY, DON GABRIEL. THE MAIN THING IS TO MAKE SURE THE STRAWBERRY IS RIPE AND NOT BRUISED OR ROTTEN. AND IF YOU GET TIRED FROM SQUATTING, YOU CAN PICK ON YOUR KNEES.
GABRIEL LEARNED QUICKLY.

AT NOON, PAPÁ INVITED GABRIEL TO JOIN US FOR LUNCH.
NOT AGAIN! WE GET THIS SAME LUNCH FROM THAT DÍAZ EVERY DAY. I AM REALLY TIRED OF THIS.
YOU CAN HAVE ONE OF MY TAQUITOS.
ONLY IF YOU TAKE ONE JELLY SANDWICH.

DO YOU HAVE A FAMILY, DON GABRIEL?
YES, AND I MISS THEM A LOT. ESPECIALLY MY THREE KIDS.
HOW OLD ARE THEY?
FIVE, THREE, AND TWO. AND YOU, DON PANCHO, HOW MANY DO YOU HAVE?
A HANDFUL! FIVE BOYS AND A GIRL, ALL LIVING AT HOME!

YOU'RE LUCKY. YOU GET TO SEE THEM EVERY DAY. I HAVEN'T SEEN MINE FOR MONTHS.
I DIDN'T WANT TO LEAVE THEM IN MORELOS, BUT I HAD NO CHOICE. WE HAVE TO EAT.
I'D SEND THEM MORE MONEY, BUT AFTER I PAY DÍAZ FOR ROOM AND BOARD AND TRANSPORTATION, LITTLE IS LEFT. HE IS A CROOK. OVERCHARGES FOR EVERYTHING.

THAT EVENING, AND FOR SEVERAL DAYS AFTER, I WAS TOO TIRED TO PLAY OUTSIDE. BUT AS I GOT MORE AND MORE USED TO PICKING STRAWBERRIES, I BEGAN TO PLAY KICK-THE-CAN AGAIN.
THE GAME WAS ALWAYS THE SAME. WE WOULD PLAY BY CARLOS'S RULES AND HE REFUSED TO LET MANUELITO PLAY.

WORK WAS ALWAYS THE SAME TOO. WE WOULD PICK FROM SIX O'CLOCK IN THE MORNING UNTIL SIX IN THE EVENING.
EVEN THOUGH THE DAYS WERE LONG, I LOOKED FORWARD TO HAVING LUNCH WITH GABRIEL...
...AND HEARING HIM TELL STORIES AND TALK ABOUT MEXICO.

ONE SUNDAY, NEAR THE END OF THE STRAWBERRY SEASON, ITO SENT GABRIEL AND ME TO WORK FOR A SHARECROPPER WHO WAS SICK AND NEEDED EXTRA HELP THAT DAY.

AS SOON AS WE ARRIVED, MR. DÍAZ BEGAN GIVING ME ORDERS.

LISTEN, HUERQUITO!

I WANT YOU TO HOE WEEDS. BUT FIRST GIVE ME AND GABRIEL A HAND.

TIE THIS AROUND YOUR WAIST. I WANT YOU TO TILL THE FURROWS.
I CAN'T DO THAT.
WHAT DO YOU MEAN, YOU "CAN'T"?
IN MY COUNTRY, OXEN PULL PLOWS, NOT MEN. I AM NOT AN ANIMAL.
WELL, THIS ISN'T YOUR COUNTRY, IDIOT! EITHER DO WHAT I SAY, OR I'LL HAVE YOU FIRED!
DON'T DO THAT, PLEASE. I HAVE A FAMILY TO FEED.

I DON'T GIVE A DAMN ABOUT YOUR FAMILY!

KICK

SHOVE

PANT
PANT
DON'T BE STUPID... REMEMBER, THINK ABOUT YOUR FAMILY!

AS WE WATCHED
DÍAZ DRIVE AWAY,
I FELT SCARED.

THAT
DÍAZ IS A
COWARD.

HE THINKS HE'S A BIG
MAN BECAUSE HE RUNS THE
BRACERO CAMP. HE'S NOTHING
BUT A LEECH! AND NOW HE TRIES
TO TREAT ME LIKE AN ANIMAL.

HE CAN CHEAT ME
OUT OF MY MONEY.
HE CAN FIRE ME.

BUT HE CAN'T FORCE ME TO
DO WHAT ISN'T RIGHT. HE
CAN'T TAKE AWAY MY DIGNITY.
THAT HE CAN'T DO!

#@!!*
ALL DAY WHILE GABRIEL AND
I HOED WEEDS, I KEPT THINKING
ABOUT WHAT HAD HAPPENED. IT
MADE ME ANGRY AND SAD.

WHEN WE GOT HOME FROM WORK, I WANTED TO BE ALONE, BUT MY BROTHERS WOULD NOT LET ME.
COME ON, GUYS, LET'S PLAY!

YOU HEARD CARLOS— LET'S PLAY!
HE DIDN'T MEAN ME.
YES, YOU TOO!

IS IT TRUE, CARLOS?
NO WAY!
IF MANUELITO DOESN'T PLAY, I WON'T EITHER.

MANUELITO

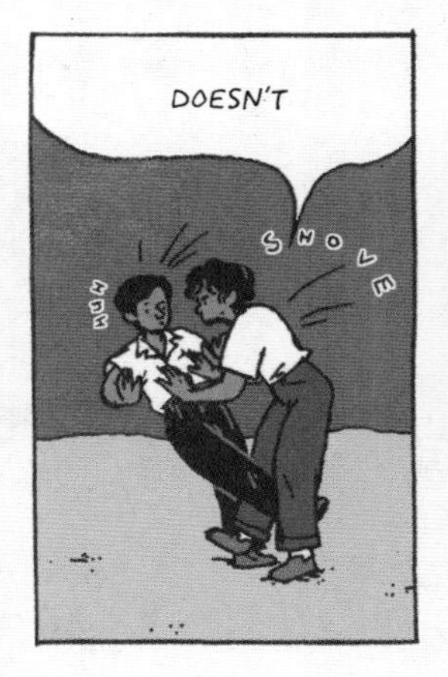
DOESN'T
SHOVE

PLAY!
THUD

YOU CAN PUSH ME AROUND, BUT YOU CAN'T FORCE ME TO PLAY!

PTOO
CARLOS COCKED HIS HEAD AND SPAT ON THE GROUND.

OKAY, MANUELITO CAN PLAY.

THE FOLLOWING MORNING, ITO TOLD US THAT THE CONTRATISTA HAD GOTTEN GABRIEL FIRED AND THAT GABRIEL WAS SENT BACK TO MEXICO. I FELT AS IF SOMEONE HAD KICKED ME IN THE STOMACH.
WHAT'S THE MATTER, PANCHITO? YOU'RE TOO SLOW. YOU NEED TO SPEED IT UP.
I KEEP THINKING ABOUT GABRIEL.

SOMEDAY DÍAZ WILL PAY FOR THAT—IF NOT IN THIS LIFE, IN THE NEXT ONE.

GABRIEL DID WHAT HE HAD TO DO.

WITH PAPÁ'S HELP, I GOT THROUGH THAT LONG DAY.
WHEN WE GOT HOME, I WANTED TO BE LEFT ALONE, BUT...
KNOCK KNOCK
PLEASE, JUST ONE GAME.
OKAY, JUST ONE.

WHEN I GOT TO THE CAN, I KICKED IT WITH ALL MY MIGHT.
THAT WAS THE LAST TIME I PLAYED THE GAME.

TO HAVE
and
TO HOLD

AS USUAL, AFTER STRAWBERRY SEASON WAS OVER, PAPÁ DECIDED TO MOVE TO THE SAN JOAQUIN VALLEY TO PICK GRAPES.
PAPÁ DID NOT WANT US TO LIVE IN MR. SULLIVAN'S OLD GARAGE IN FRESNO AGAIN. SO WE HEADED FOR OROSI, A SMALL TOWN A FEW MILES FROM FRESNO.
PAPÁ HAD HEARD THAT A GRAPE GROWER THERE NAMED MR. PATRINI HAD NICE PLACES FOR FARM WORKERS TO LIVE.

WE LEFT SANTA MARIA IN SEPTEMBER, THE WEEK SCHOOL STARTED.
AS WE PASSED MAIN STREET, I PULLED OUT MY PENNY COLLECTION, TOOK MY NOTEPAD OUT OF MY SHIRT POCKET, AND HELD BOTH AS I WONDERED WHAT OROSI WOULD BE LIKE.

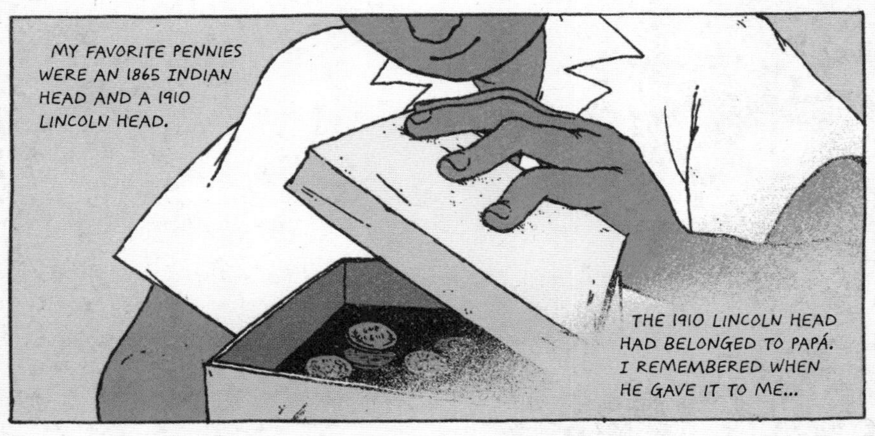
MY FAVORITE PENNIES WERE AN 1865 INDIAN HEAD AND A 1910 LINCOLN HEAD.
THE 1910 LINCOLN HEAD HAD BELONGED TO PAPÁ. I REMEMBERED WHEN HE GAVE IT TO ME...

DO YOU KNOW HOW OLD THIS COIN IS?

NO, PAPÁ.
IT WAS MADE THE YEAR I WAS BORN, THE SAME YEAR THE REVOLUTION STARTED.
WHAT REVOLUTION?

THE MEXICAN REVOLUTION. I DON'T KNOW THE WHOLE STORY. I DIDN'T GO TO SCHOOL...
...BUT WHAT I KNOW I LEARNED FROM LISTENING TO CORRIDOS AND TO YOUR ABUELITA ESTEFANÍA.

SHE TOLD ME THAT DURING THAT TIME, MANY OF THE RICH HACENDADOS TREATED THE CAMPESINOS LIKE SLAVES.

DID ABUELITO HILARIO FIGHT IN THE REVOLUTION?
NO, MI'JO. MY FATHER DIED SIX MONTHS AFTER I WAS BORN.
BUT YOUR ABUELITA FAVORED THE REVOLUTION, JUST LIKE ALL POOR PEOPLE DID.
I ALSO HEARD THE HACENDADOS BURIED THEIR MONEY AND JEWELS IN THE GROUND TO HIDE THEM FROM THE REVOLUTIONARIES.
MANY OF THOSE TREASURES HAVE NEVER BEEN FOUND.
BUT THEY SAY YELLOWISH-RED FLAMES SHOOT FROM WHERE TREASURE IS BURIED...AND YOU CAN SEE THE BLAZES FROM FAR AWAY AT NIGHT.
I DON'T KNOW IF THAT'S TRUE, BUT THAT'S WHAT THEY SAY.

YOU CAN HAVE THE PENNY, PANCHITO. THIS WAY YOU'LL NEVER FORGET THE YEAR I WAS BORN.
AND, IF YOU KEEP ON SAVING YOUR PENNIES, YOU'LL HAVE YOUR OWN TREASURE.

THAT'S WHEN I STARTED COLLECTING PENNIES. I LIKED THE OLDER ONES BEST.

UNITED STATES OF AMERICA
AS WE MADE OUR WAY UP THE SAN LUIS OBISPO GRADE, I TOOK OUT MY 1865 INDIAN HEAD COIN.

CARL HAD GIVEN IT TO ME WHEN I WAS IN THE FIFTH GRADE IN CORCORAN.
WHEN WE FOUND OUT THAT WE BOTH COLLECTED COINS, WE BECAME BEST FRIENDS.
WE MADE SURE WE GOT ON THE SAME TEAM WHEN WE PLAYED BALL DURING RECESS...AND WE ATE OUR LUNCH TOGETHER EVERY DAY.

ONE FRIDAY AFTER SCHOOL, CARL INVITED ME TO HIS HOME TO SEE HIS COIN COLLECTION.

HIS HOUSE WAS ONLY THREE BLOCKS AWAY.
C'MON!

I HAD NEVER BEEN INSIDE A REAL HOUSE BEFORE.
THE RUG UNDER MY FEET FELT LIKE A SACK FULL OF COTTON. THE LIVING ROOM WAS WARM AND AS BIG AS THE ONE-ROOM CABIN WE LIVED IN. THE LIGHT WAS SOFT AND SOOTHING.

CARL HAD HIS OWN BED AND HIS OWN DESK.
THESE ARE MY PENNIES!

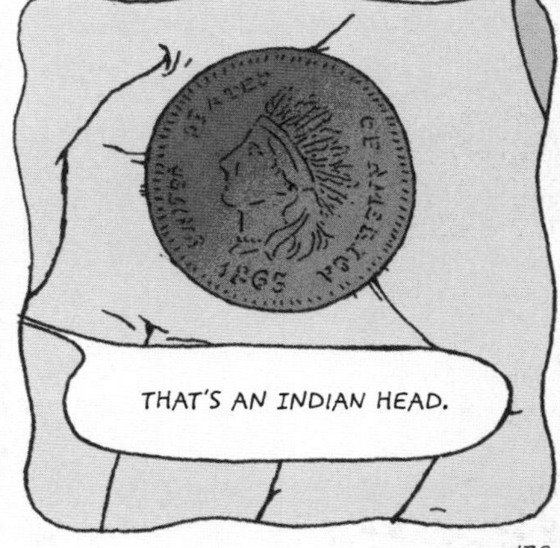
1865
THAT'S AN INDIAN HEAD.

I THOUGHT ALL PENNIES WERE LINCOLN HEADS!
OH, NO! SEE? I HAVE LOTS OF INDIAN HEADS.

THE OLDEST IS FROM 1865!

I'LL GIVE YOU ANY OF MY LINCOLN PENNIES FOR ONE INDIAN HEAD.
YOU DON'T HAVE TO. I'LL GIVE YOU ONE. PICK THE ONE YOU WANT.

I PICKED THE OLDEST ONE.
THANKS!

WHEN CAN I COME BY YOUR HOUSE AND SEE YOUR COLLECTION?
HIS QUESTION TOOK ME BY SURPRISE.
I LIVE TOO FAR. I'LL BRING MY COLLECTION TO SCHOOL. IT'S NOT MUCH.
THAT'S OKAY—I'D LIKE TO SEE IT ANYWAY!

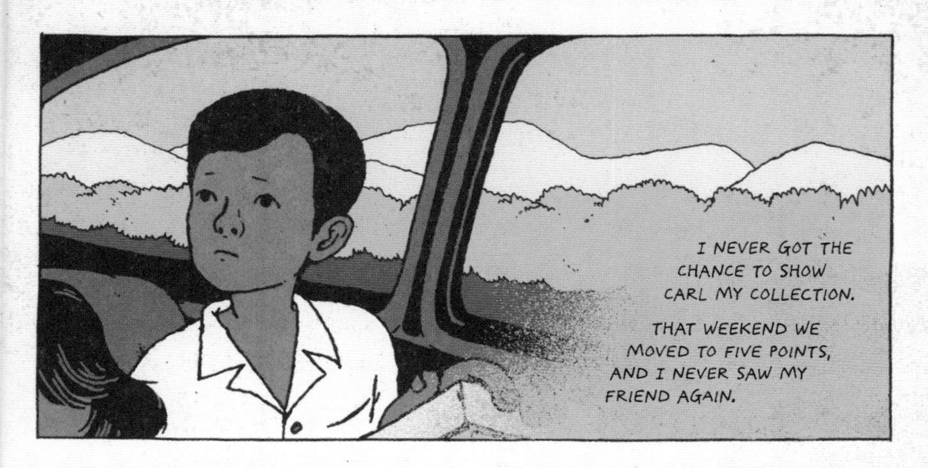
I NEVER GOT THE CHANCE TO SHOW CARL MY COLLECTION.
THAT WEEKEND WE MOVED TO FIVE POINTS, AND I NEVER SAW MY FRIEND AGAIN.

ORO-SI. ORO MEANT "GOLD" IN SPANISH, AND SÍ MEANT EITHER "YES" OR "IF."
BASED ON WHAT PAPÁ SAID, I FIGURED IT MEANT "YES" IN THIS CASE.
WHAT DOES OROSI MEAN?
I AM NOT SURE, MI'JO. BUT I HAVE A FEELING WE'RE GOING TO LIKE IT THERE.

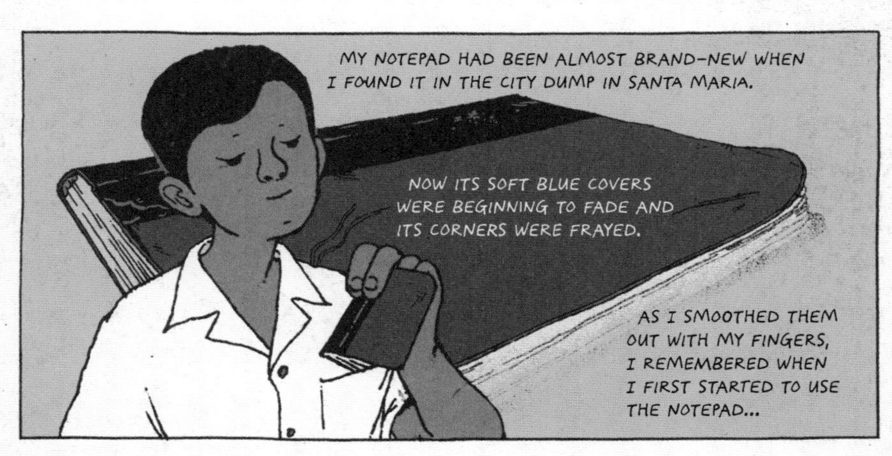
MY NOTEPAD HAD BEEN ALMOST BRAND-NEW WHEN I FOUND IT IN THE CITY DUMP IN SANTA MARIA.
NOW ITS SOFT BLUE COVERS WERE BEGINNING TO FADE AND ITS CORNERS WERE FRAYED.
AS I SMOOTHED THEM OUT WITH MY FINGERS, I REMEMBERED WHEN I FIRST STARTED TO USE THE NOTEPAD...

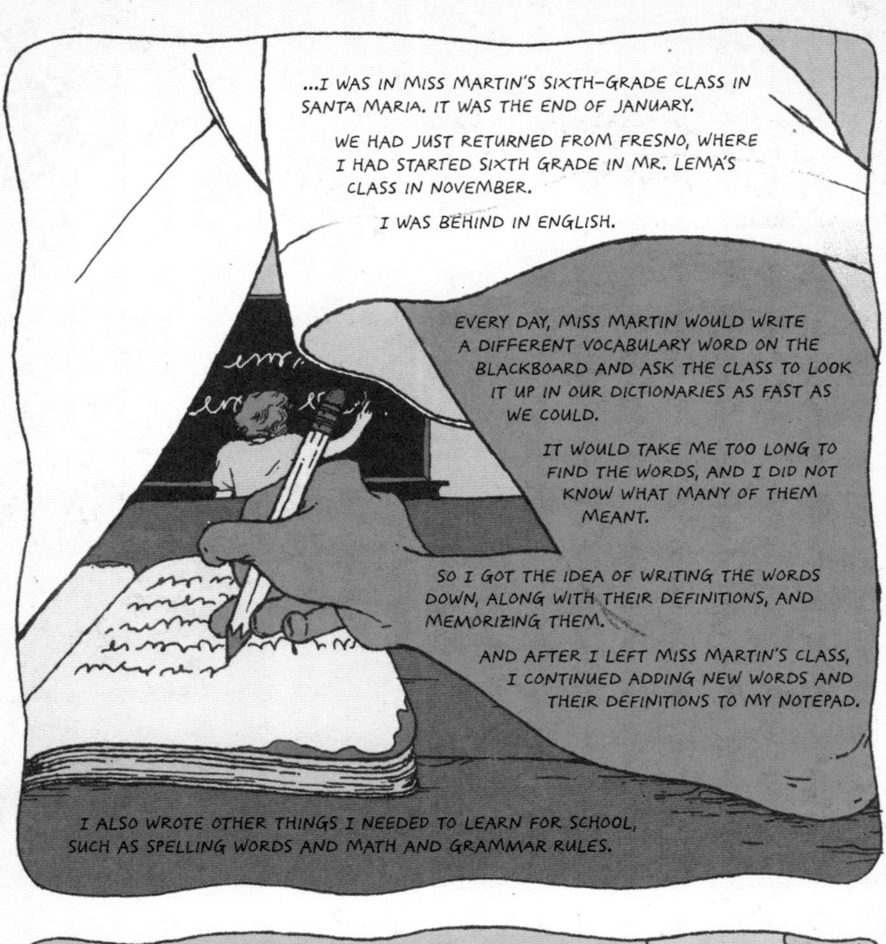
...I WAS IN MISS MARTIN'S SIXTH-GRADE CLASS IN SANTA MARIA. IT WAS THE END OF JANUARY.
WE HAD JUST RETURNED FROM FRESNO, WHERE I HAD STARTED SIXTH GRADE IN MR. LEMA'S CLASS IN NOVEMBER.
I WAS BEHIND IN ENGLISH.
EVERY DAY, MISS MARTIN WOULD WRITE A DIFFERENT VOCABULARY WORD ON THE BLACKBOARD AND ASK THE CLASS TO LOOK IT UP IN OUR DICTIONARIES AS FAST AS WE COULD.
IT WOULD TAKE ME TOO LONG TO FIND THE WORDS, AND I DID NOT KNOW WHAT MANY OF THEM MEANT.
SO I GOT THE IDEA OF WRITING THE WORDS DOWN, ALONG WITH THEIR DEFINITIONS, AND MEMORIZING THEM.
AND AFTER I LEFT MISS MARTIN'S CLASS, I CONTINUED ADDING NEW WORDS AND THEIR DEFINITIONS TO MY NOTEPAD.
I ALSO WROTE OTHER THINGS I NEEDED TO LEARN FOR SCHOOL, SUCH AS SPELLING WORDS AND MATH AND GRAMMAR RULES.

I CARRIED THE NOTEPAD IN MY SHIRT POCKET AND, WHILE I WORKED IN THE FIELDS, MEMORIZED THE INFORMATION I HAD WRITTEN.
I TOOK MY LIBRITO WITH ME WHEREVER I WENT.

AFTER TRAVELING FOR ABOUT FIVE HOURS, WE ARRIVED AT OUR NEW HOME. AN OLD YELLOW WOODEN HOUSE, ABOUT 15 MILES OUTSIDE OROSI.

MR. PATRINI, THE OWNER, TOLD US OUR NEW HOME IN OROSI WAS SEVENTY YEARS OLD.
WE COULD NOT USE THE SECOND LEVEL BECAUSE THE FLOORS WERE UNSTABLE. BUT THE FIRST FLOOR HAD TWO ROOMS AND A KITCHEN.
BEHIND THE HOUSE WERE A LARGE BARN AND HUNDREDS OF VINEYARDS.

IT DID NOT TAKE
LONG TO SETTLE IN.

PAPÁ, MAMÁ, AND RORRA TOOK ONE ROOM; ROBERTO, TRAMPITA, TORITO, RUBÉN, AND I MOVED INTO THE OTHER.

AFTER PUTTING AWAY OUR FEW THINGS, I LOOKED AT MY PENNIES TO MAKE SURE THEY WERE NOT RUBBING AGAINST ONE ANOTHER.
CAN I HAVE ONE?
ONE WHAT, RORRA?
A PENNY.
NOT ONE OF THESE. THESE ARE SPECIAL.

THAT EVENING I CHECKED ON MY PENNIES AND MY NOTEPAD AGAIN.
AFTER OUR PRAYERS, I HAD TROUBLE FALLING ASLEEP.
MY LITTLE BROTHERS MUST HAVE BEEN EXCITED TOO, BECAUSE THEY STARTED WHISPERING AND GIGGLING.
I CAN'T BELIEVE WE ARE LIVING IN A HOUSE.

LISTEN. I HEAR LA LLORONA WEEPING UPSTAIRS.
I DON'T HEAR ANYTHING. YOU ARE JUST TRYING TO SCARE US.
JUST BE QUIET AND YOU'LL HEAR HER.
THERE WAS DEAD SILENCE THE REST OF THE NIGHT.

THE NEXT DAY, BEFORE SUNRISE, PAPÁ, ROBERTO, TRAMPITA, AND I WENT TO PICK GRAPES FOR MR. PATRINI.
I TOOK MY NOTEPAD WITH ME. I WANTED TO LEARN SOME SPELLING RULES WHILE I WORKED, BUT I COULDN'T.

THE ANGRY, BLISTERING SUN DID NOT LET ME.
BY TEN O'CLOCK, MY SHIRT WAS SOAKING WET.

I CAREFULLY REMOVED THE NOTEPAD FROM MY SHIRT POCKET AND TOOK IT TO THE CARCACHITA SO IT WOULDN'T GET DIRTY AND WET.

BY THE END OF THE DAY, MY WHOLE BODY WAS COVERED WITH DUST. MY ARMS AND HANDS LOOKED AS IF THEY WERE MADE OF CLAY.
I SCRAPED THE MUDDY LAYER OFF THEM WITH THE HOOKED KNIFE I USED FOR CUTTING GRAPES.

AT SUNDOWN, MAMÁ AND RORRA DROVE TO THE STORE WHILE...

...PAPÁ, ROBERTO, TRAMPITA, AND I STRIPPED DOWN TO OUR UNDERWEAR AND BATHED IN A TROUGH BEHIND THE HOUSE.

DID YOU GET ANY PENNIES IN CHANGE?
ONE.

1939!
CAN I HAVE IT?

OF COURSE, MI'JITO.

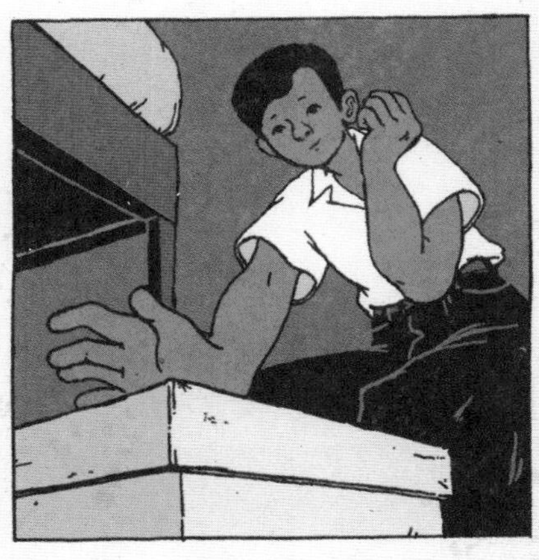

NO, THEY HAVE
TO BE HERE!

RORRA! DID YOU
TAKE MY PENNIES?
IF YOU DID,
GIVE THEM
TO ME!
CALM DOWN,
PANCHITO.

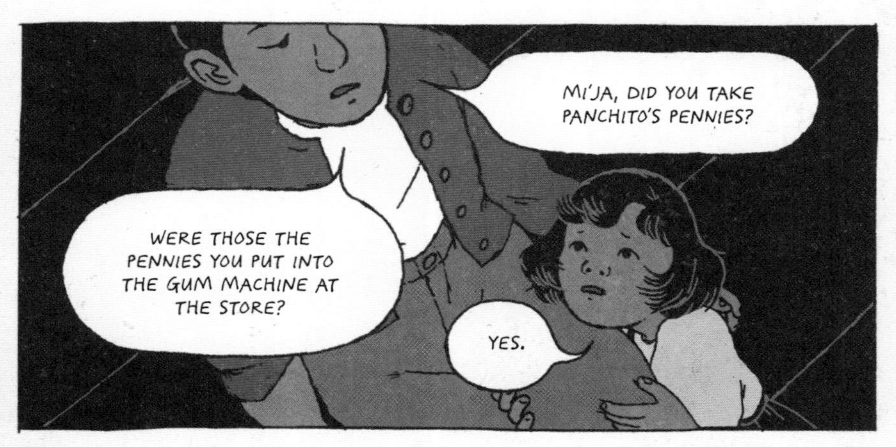
MI'JA, DID YOU TAKE
PANCHITO'S PENNIES?
WERE THOSE THE
PENNIES YOU PUT INTO
THE GUM MACHINE AT
THE STORE?
YES.

WHAM
MY HEART DROPPED TO MY STOMACH. IT FELT AS IF MY FACE WERE ON FIRE. EVERYTHING BLURRED.

I KNOW HOW DISAPPOINTED YOU ARE, MI'JITO.
BUT YOUR SISTER IS ONLY FOUR YEARS OLD.

LET ME TELL YOU A STORY I HEARD WHEN I WAS A LITTLE GIRL.

ONCE, THERE WAS A VERY SMART ANT WHO SAVED HER PENNIES AND BECAME RICH.

EVERY ANIMAL AROUND WANTED TO MARRY HER. BUT THE ANIMALS FRIGHTENED HER.
THE CAT MEWED TOO MUCH,
THE PARROT TALKED TOO MUCH,
THE DOG BARKED TOO LOUD,
AND THE BULL AND GOAT SCARED HER.

BUT NOT A LITTLE BROWN MOUSE NAMED EL RATONCITO.
HE WAS QUIET, INTELLIGENT, POLITE, AND MANNERLY.
THEY GOT MARRIED AND WERE VERY HAPPY.

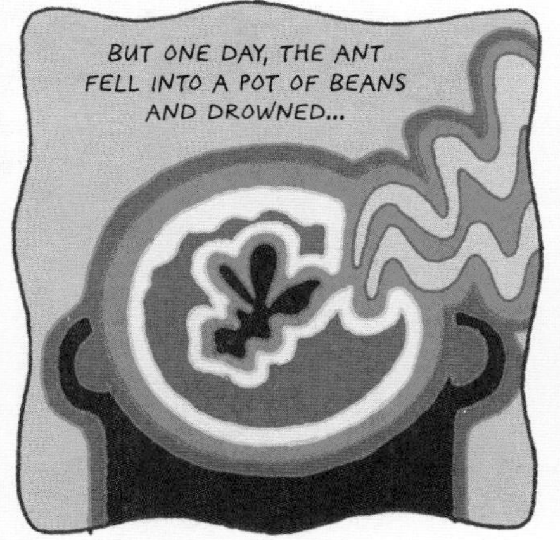
BUT ONE DAY, THE ANT FELL INTO A POT OF BEANS AND DROWNED...

...LEAVING EL RATONCITO WITH A LOT OF PENNIES BUT TERRIBLY SAD AND LONELY.

SO YOU SEE, MI'JITO, RORRA IS MORE THAN THE PENNIES.
DON'T BE TOO HARD ON YOUR LITTLE SISTER.

MAMÁ'S STORY CALMED ME DOWN A LITTLE, BUT I WAS STILL ANGRY WITH RORRA.
THE FOLLOWING MORNING, MAMÁ AND I COVERED MY NOTEPAD WITH WAXED PAPER TO KEEP IT CLEAN.

AS I PICKED GRAPES, I WENT OVER SPELLING RULES IN MY MIND, LOOKING AT MY NOTES ONLY WHEN I HAD TO.

ON OUR WAY HOME, WE STOPPED AT A GAS STATION TO GET KEROSENE FOR OUR STOVE.

PANCHITO, THIS DOES NOT SMELL LIKE KEROSENE. IT SMELLS LIKE GASOLINE.
YOU BETTER GO TELL PAPÁ.

I'M SURE IT'S FINE, MI'JO. IT'S PROBABLY CHEAP KEROSENE.

PAPÁ SAID IT'S OKAY.
OKAY.

INDEPENDENCE
SAFETY

¡AY, DIOS MÍO!
VIEJO, THE KITCHEN IS ON FIRE!!!!!
GET OUT! OUT, OUT!

!

THE INSTANT I SAW THE SILVER METAL BOX WHERE PAPÁ KEPT OUR SAVINGS, I THOUGHT OF MY NOTEPAD.
¡MI LIBRITO!
ARE YOU CRAZY?
¡YA! ¡NO SEAS TONTO, PANCHO!

BY THE TIME THE FIREMEN CAME, THE HOUSE HAD BURNED DOWN COMPLETELY.

LET'S STAY IN THE BARN TONIGHT. TOMORROW WE'LL LOOK FOR ANOTHER PLACE.

COME ON, PANCHITO.

WE'RE SAFE.
AND WE HAVE ONE ANOTHER, GRACIAS A DIOS.
YES...BUT WHAT ABOUT MY LIBRITO?

IT'S GONE. JUST LIKE MY PENNIES.
DO YOU KNOW WHAT WAS IN YOUR LIBRITO?

YES...
WELL...IF YOU KNOW WHAT WAS IN YOUR LIBRITO, THEN IT'S NOT ALL LOST.

I HEARD MAMÁ'S WORDS BUT DID NOT UNDERSTAND WHAT SHE MEANT UNTIL A FEW DAYS LATER.

WE HAD MOVED TO A LABOR CAMP AND WERE PICKING GRAPES AGAIN FOR MR. PATRINI.

IT WAS A SCORCHING DAY. MY CLOTHES WERE DRENCHED IN SWEAT.
I CROUCHED UNDERNEATH THE VINES FOR SHADE, BUT THE HEAT PIERCED RIGHT THROUGH.
I RECALLED THE FIRE AND PLACED MY RIGHT HAND OVER MY SHIRT POCKET. IT WAS EMPTY.
I STARTED THINKING ABOUT CARL, MY PENNIES, THE HOUSE.
THEN, FOR A LONG TIME, I THOUGHT ABOUT MY LIBRITO AND WHAT MAMÁ HAD SAID.

I COULD SEE IN MY MIND VOCABULARY WORDS, TIMES TABLES, AND SPELLING AND GRAMMAR RULES THAT I HAD WRITTEN IN MY NOTEPAD.

I KNEW EVERYTHING IN MY LIBRITO BY HEART.

MAMÁ WAS RIGHT. IT WAS NOT ALL LOST.

Moving Still

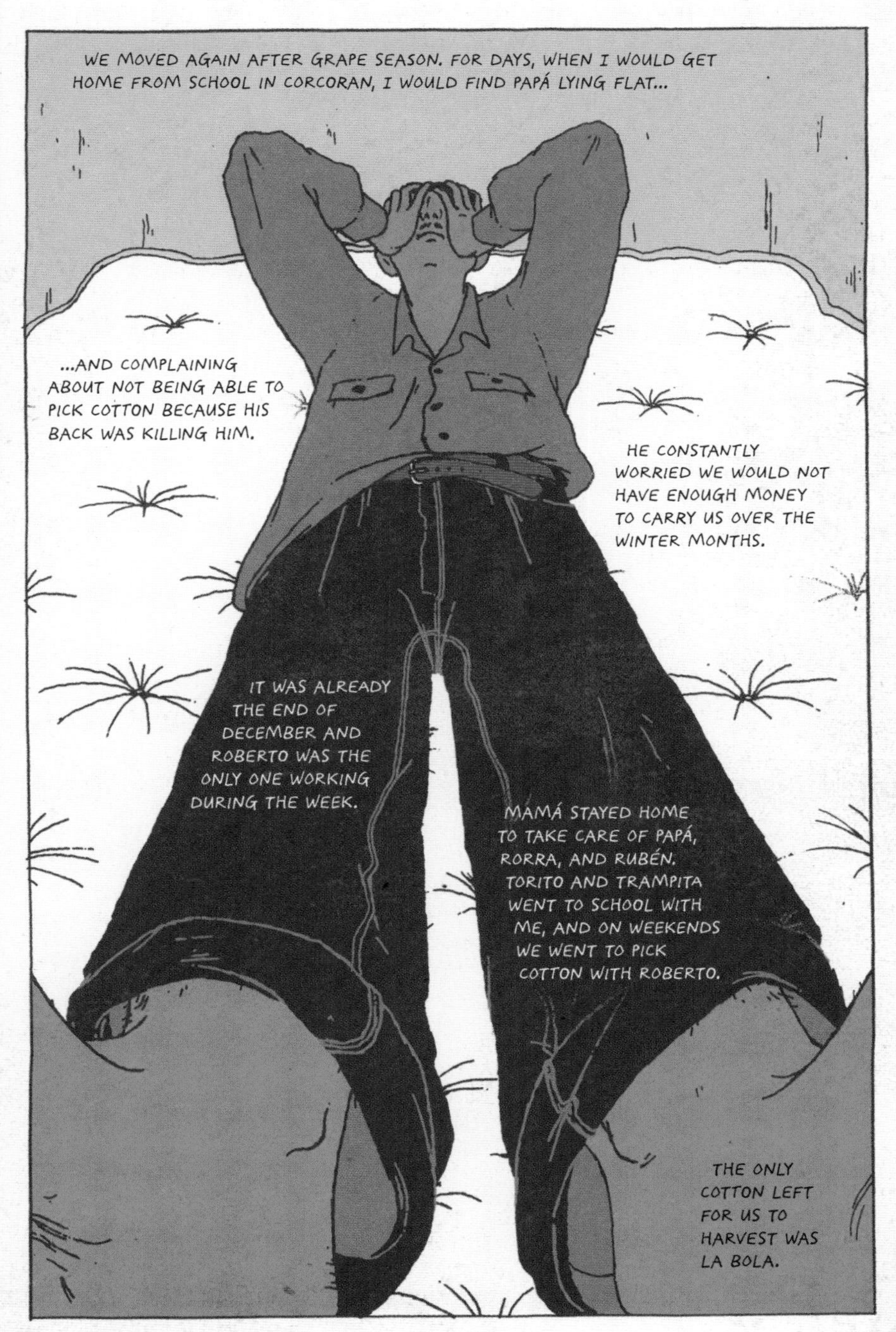
WE MOVED AGAIN AFTER GRAPE SEASON. FOR DAYS, WHEN I WOULD GET HOME FROM SCHOOL IN CORCORAN, I WOULD FIND PAPÁ LYING FLAT...
...AND COMPLAINING ABOUT NOT BEING ABLE TO PICK COTTON BECAUSE HIS BACK WAS KILLING HIM.
HE CONSTANTLY WORRIED WE WOULD NOT HAVE ENOUGH MONEY TO CARRY US OVER THE WINTER MONTHS.
IT WAS ALREADY THE END OF DECEMBER AND ROBERTO WAS THE ONLY ONE WORKING DURING THE WEEK.
MAMÁ STAYED HOME TO TAKE CARE OF PAPÁ, RORRA, AND RUBÉN. TORITO AND TRAMPITA WENT TO SCHOOL WITH ME, AND ON WEEKENDS WE WENT TO PICK COTTON WITH ROBERTO.
THE ONLY COTTON LEFT FOR US TO HARVEST WAS LA BOLA.

BUT ONE DAY WHEN I GOT HOME FROM SCHOOL, PAPÁ DID NOT COMPLAIN ABOUT ANYTHING. NOT EVEN HIS BACK.
MI'JO, ARE YOU ALL RIGHT?
SÍ, PAPÁ.

¡GRACIAS A DIOS! LA MIGRA SWEPT THROUGH THE CAMPS ABOUT AN HOUR AGO.

I DIDN'T KNOW IF THE IMMIGRATION OFFICERS SEARCHED YOUR SCHOOL, TOO.

THE WORD "MIGRA" EVOKED FEAR EVER SINCE AN IMMIGRATION RAID IN TENT CITY IN SANTA MARIA.
IT HAD BEEN A SATURDAY WHEN WE HAD HEARD,
"¡LA MIGRA! ¡LA MIGRA!"

WE WERE LUCKY MAMÁ AND
ROBERTO HAD GONE TO TOWN
TO BUY GROCERIES.

PAPÁ SHOWED THE OFFICERS THE GREEN CARD
THAT ITO HAD HELPED HIM GET. THEY DID NOT
ASK ANYTHING ELSE, AND THEY DID NOT ASK
ABOUT TRAMPITA OR ME.

WHEN ROBERTO CAME HOME FROM WORK THAT EVENING, PAPÁ AND MAMÁ WERE RELIEVED TO SEE HIM.
YOU DIDN'T SEE LA MIGRA?
IT CAME TO OUR CAMP BUT MISSED US.

IT DIDN'T COME TO THE FIELD.
SO YOU DIDN'T GO OUT WITH LA MIGRA.
NO, PAPÁ, SHE'S NOT MY TYPE.

THEN PAPÁ GREW SERIOUS AND REPEATED THE WORDS I HAD ALREADY MEMORIZED.

YOU HAVE TO BE CAREFUL.

YOU CAN'T TELL A SOUL YOU WERE BORN IN MEXICO. YOU CAN'T TRUST ANYONE.
NOT EVEN YOUR BEST FRIENDS. IF THEY KNOW, THEY CAN TURN YOU IN.
NOW, WHERE WERE YOU BORN, PANCHITO?
COLTON, CALIFORNIA
GOOD, MI'JO.

ROBERTO HANDED PAPÁ THE MONEY HE HAD EARNED THAT DAY.
I AM USELESS.

I CAN'T WORK... CAN'T FEED MY FAMILY... I CAN'T EVEN PROTECT YOU FROM LA MIGRA.
DON'T SAY THAT, PAPÁ.

PAPÁ ASKED ME TO BRING HIM THE SMALL METAL BOX WHERE HE KEPT OUR SAVINGS.
IF I WORK IN SANTA MARIA INSTEAD OF CORCORAN, WE MIGHT BE ABLE TO GET THROUGH THIS WINTER WITH WHAT WE'VE SAVED.
BUT WHAT IF MY BACK WON'T LET ME?

DON'T WORRY, PAPÁ. PANCHITO COULD THIN LETTUCE AND TOP CARROTS IN SANTA MARIA.

ROBERTO'S RIGHT, VIEJO. LET'S LEAVE.
BESIDES, IMMIGRATION MAY COME AROUND AGAIN. IT'S SAFER IN SANTA MARIA.

YOU'RE RIGHT. WE'LL GO BACK TO BONETTI RANCH. TOMORROW MORNING.
WE RETURNED TO BONETTI RANCH IN SANTA MARIA EVERY YEAR AFTER THE COTTON SEASON WAS OVER.
WE HAD LIVED THERE IN BARRACKS EIGHT MONTHS OUT OF THE YEAR, FROM JANUARY THROUGH AUGUST, EVER SINCE TENT CITY HAD BEEN TORN DOWN BY THE SANTA BARBARA COUNTY PUBLIC HEALTH DEPARTMENT A YEAR AFTER TORITO GOT SICK.
MOST OF THE RESIDENTS WERE MEXICAN FIELD LABORERS WHO WERE AMERICAN CITIZENS OR HAD IMMIGRANT VISAS LIKE PAPÁ.
THIS MADE THE RANCH RELATIVELY SAFE FROM BORDER PATROL RAIDS.

I WAS SO EXCITED ABOUT GOING BACK TO BONETTI RANCH EARLY THAT I WAS THE FIRST ONE UP THE FOLLOWING MORNING.
ROBERTO AND TRAMPITA WERE EXCITED TOO. I IMAGINED THIS WAS HOW IT FELT TO GO AWAY ON VACATION.

PAPÁ COULD NOT DRIVE BECAUSE OF HIS BACK PAIN, SO ROBERTO DROVE.

THE TRIP TOOK ABOUT FIVE HOURS, BUT IT SEEMED LIKE FIVE DAYS TO ME.

CAN'T YOU GO FASTER?
SURE, IF YOU WANT US TO GET A TICKET.
THAT'S ALL WE NEED. IF THAT HAPPENS, WE MIGHT AS WELL TURN OURSELVES IN TO LA MIGRA!

LET'S STOP FOR LUNCH.

WE CAN EAT IN THE CAR, MAMÁ.

WHAT ABOUT ROBERTO? HE CAN'T EAT AND DRIVE.

BRAAAAKE

I GOBBLED MY TWO TACOS, BOTH WITH EGG AND CHORIZO, AND SIGNALED TO ROBERTO TO HURRY.
TUG TUG
¡YA, PUES! PANCHITO. I'M ALMOST FINISHED.

THE CLOSER WE GOT TO SANTA MARIA, THE MORE EXCITED I BECAME BECAUSE I KNEW WHERE WE WERE GOING TO LIVE FOR THE NEXT EIGHT MONTHS.
SOON I WOULD GET TO SEE MY CLASSMATES IN THE EIGHTH GRADE AT EL CAMINO JUNIOR HIGH.
I HAD NOT SEEN THEM SINCE LAST JUNE.
I WONDER IF THEY'LL REMEMBER ME?

WE'RE HERE!
SE HAN VUELTO LOCOS.

HOTEL
WHEN WE GOT TO MAIN STREET, ROBERTO TURNED LEFT AND DROVE EAST FOR ABOUT TEN MILES.

ALONG THE WAY, I KEPT POINTING OUT PLACES I RECOGNIZED:
LOOK!

MAIN STREET SCHOOL,

KRESS, THE FIVE-AND-DIME STORE,

THE TEXACO GAS STATION WHERE WE GOT OUR DRINKING WATER,
TEXACO

AND THE HOSPITAL WHERE TORITO HAD STAYED WHEN HE GOT SICK.

WE THEN CROSSED SUEY ROAD, WHICH MARKED THE END OF THE CITY LIMITS AND THE BEGINNING OF HUNDREDS OF ACRES OF RECENTLY PLANTED LETTUCE AND CARROTS.
NOTHING HAD CHANGED IN BONETTI RANCH FROM THE YEAR BEFORE. DOZENS OF STRAY DOGS GREETED US.
THEY SLEPT UNDERNEATH THE DWELLINGS AND ATE WHATEVER THEY FOUND IN THE GARBAGE.
I FELT SORRY FOR THEM AND WONDERED IF THEY WERE AS BOTHERED BY THE FLEAS THAT PLAGUED THEM AS WE WERE BY THE LITTLE BUGS THAT INVADED OUR BEDS AT NIGHT.
LOOKING LIKE VICTIMS OF A WAR, THE DWELLINGS HAD BROKEN WINDOWS, PARTS OF WALLS MISSING, AND LARGE HOLES IN THE ROOFS.
SCATTERED THROUGHOUT THE RANCH WERE OLD, RUSTY PIECES OF FARM MACHINERY.

WE RENTED AND MOVED INTO THE SAME BARRACK WE HAD LIVED IN THE PREVIOUS YEAR...
...NEXT TO OUR HOUSE WERE EMPTY OIL BARRELS THAT SERVED AS GARBAGE CANS FOR THE RESIDENTS.

BEHIND OUR BARRACK WAS THE SHARED OUTHOUSE, WHICH WOULD SHIFT ON RAINY DAYS.

WE COVERED THE GAPS BETWEEN WALLBOARDS WITH PAPER, PAINTED THE INSIDE...

...AND COVERED THE FLOOR USING PAINT AND PIECES OF LINOLEUM WE FOUND AT THE CITY DUMP.
WE HAD ELECTRICITY.

WE COULD NOT DRINK THE WATER—IT WAS OILY AND SMELLED LIKE SULFUR—BUT WE USED IT FOR BATHING.
WE HEATED IT ON THE STOVE AND POURED IT INTO THE LARGE ALUMINUM CONTAINER THAT WE USED FOR A BATHTUB.

FOR DRINKING WATER, WE TOOK OUR FIVE-GALLON BOTTLE AND FILLED IT AT THE TEXACO STATION DOWNTOWN.

ALONG THE FRONT EDGE OF OUR BARRACK, ROBERTO PLANTED GERANIUMS.

AROUND THEM, HE BUILT A FENCE

AND PAINTED IT, ALSO USING SUPPLIES FROM THE CITY DUMP.

THE WEEK AFTER WE ARRIVED, WE ENROLLED IN SCHOOL.
EVEN THOUGH THIS WAS MY FIRST TIME IN THE EIGHTH GRADE AT EL CAMINO JUNIOR HIGH, I DID NOT FEEL NERVOUS.
ROBERTO STARTED TENTH GRADE AT SANTA MARIA HIGH.
TRAMPITA AND TORITO RESUMED ELEMENTARY SCHOOL AT MAIN STREET SCHOOL.

I REMEMBERED MANY OF THE KIDS IN MY CLASS. SOME HAD GROWN TALLER, ESPECIALLY THE BOYS.
I HAD STAYED THE SAME: FOUR FEET, ELEVEN INCHES. I WAS ONE OF THE SMALLEST KIDS IN THE SCHOOL.

I HAD MR. MILO FOR MATH AND SCIENCE IN THE MORNINGS...

...AND MISS EHLIS FOR ENGLISH, HISTORY, AND SOCIAL STUDIES IN THE AFTERNOONS.

I LIKED MY TWO TEACHERS. BUT I ENJOYED MR. MILO'S CLASS MORE BECAUSE I DID BETTER IN MATH.
EVERY THURSDAY MR. MILO GAVE US A QUIZ...

...AND THE FOLLOWING DAY HE ARRANGED OUR DESKS ACCORDING TO HOW WELL WE HAD DONE ON THE TEST.

SHARON ITO, THE DAUGHTER OF THE JAPANESE SHARECROPPER FOR WHOM WE PICKED STRAWBERRIES...
...SHE AND I ALTERNATED TAKING THE FIRST SEAT, THOUGH SHE SAT IN IT MORE OFTEN THAN I DID.
I WAS GLAD WE DID NOT HAVE THE SAME SEATING ARRANGEMENT FOR ENGLISH!

AS DAYS WENT BY, PAPÁ'S BACK DID NOT GET BETTER, NOR DID HIS MOOD. WHEN NOT COMPLAINING ABOUT NOT BEING ABLE TO WORK, HE LAY IN BED WITH AN EMPTY LOOK IN HIS EYES.

I DON'T THINK YOUR PAPÁ CAN WORK IN THE FIELDS ANYMORE.
WHAT ARE WE GOING TO DO?
I'VE BEEN THINKING ABOUT GETTING A JOB IN TOWN. I'M TIRED OF WORKING IN THE FIELDS.
THAT'S A GOOD IDEA! THEN WE WON'T HAVE TO MOVE TO FRESNO.
YES, A JOB THAT IS YEAR-ROUND!
MAYBE MR. SIMS CAN HELP ME.
WHO IS MR. SIMS?
THE PRINCIPAL OF MAIN STREET SCHOOL. REMEMBER? HE GAVE ME THE GREEN JACKET.
AH, SÍ. ES MUY BUENA GENTE.

SEVERAL DAYS LATER, MR. SIMS TOLD ROBERTO THAT HE HAD FOUND A JOB FOR HIM.

MY BROTHER WOULD SEE THE OWNER OF THE BUSTER BROWN SHOE STORE ON BROADWAY THAT SATURDAY AFTERNOON.

EARLY SATURDAY MORNING, ROBERTO AND I HEADED FOR WORK: THINNING LETTUCE.
AS HE DROVE, ROBERTO COULD NOT STOP TALKING ABOUT HIS NEW JOB AT THE SHOE STORE.
HIS APPOINTMENT THAT AFTERNOON SEEMED A LONG TIME AWAY.

TO MAKE THE HOURS IN THE FIELD GO BY FASTER, WE DECIDED TO CHALLENGE OURSELVES.
WE MARKED A SPOT IN OUR ROWS, A THIRD OF THE WAY IN, TO SEE IF WE COULD REACH IT WITHOUT STRAIGHTENING UP.

READY? GO!

WE...DID...IT!
BUT MY BACK IS KILLING ME.

YOU'RE GETTING OLD, PANCHITO.
CRACK

LET'S REST.

I AM TIRED OF MOVING EVERY YEAR.
ME TOO, ROBERTO. EVER WONDER WHAT WE'LL BE DOING TEN OR TWENTY YEARS FROM NOW? OR WHERE WE'LL BE LIVING?
IN SANTA MARIA, OF COURSE. I CAN'T IMAGINE LIVING ANYWHERE ELSE.
I DON'T WANT TO LIVE IN SELMA, VISALIA, BAKERSFIELD, OR CORCORAN...
I LIKE SANTA MARIA. SO IF YOU DECIDE TO LIVE HERE FOREVER, I WILL TOO.

THIS WAS OUR CHANCE TO STAY IN SANTA MARIA. NOT MOVE TO FRESNO AT THE END OF THE SUMMER TO PICK GRAPES AND MISS SCHOOL.
PERHAPS ROBERTO WILL GET ME A JOB AT THE SHOE STORE TOO.

HOW ABOUT THAT, BUSTER BROWN!

BUT THEN ROBERTO RETURNED TO PICK ME UP.

WHAT'S THE MATTER? YOU DIDN'T GET THE JOB?
NO, I GOT THE JOB, BUT NOT WORKING AT THE STORE.

DOING WHAT, THEN?

CUTTING HIS LAWN. ONCE A WEEK.

OH NO!
I'M GOING TO SEE MR. SIMS AFTER SCHOOL ON MONDAY. MAYBE HE CAN SUGGEST SOMETHING ELSE.
DON'T LOSE FAITH, PANCHITO. THINGS WILL WORK OUT.

ON MONDAY MORNING, MY MIND WAS NOT ON SCHOOL.
I HOPE HE GETS A JOB. BUT WHAT IF HE DOESN'T? NO, HE WILL.

MISS EHLIS GAVE OUR CLASS AN ASSIGNMENT I WAS NOT EXPECTING.
THIS IS THE PART OF THE DECLARATION OF INDEPENDENCE THAT I WANT YOU TO MEMORIZE.
NOW, THERE IS NO NEED TO GROAN. THE PART IS VERY SHORT.
"WE HOLD THESE TRUTHS TO BE SELF-EVIDENT, THAT ALL MEN ARE CREATED EQUAL, THAT THEY ARE ENDOWED BY THEIR CREATOR WITH CERTAIN UNALIENABLE RIGHTS, THAT AMONG THESE ARE LIFE, LIBERTY AND THE PURSUIT OF HAPPINESS.--THAT TO SECURE THESE RIGHTS, GOVERNMENTS ARE INSTITUTED AMONG MEN, DERIVING THEIR JUST POWERS FROM THE CONSENT OF THE GOVERNED..."
IT'S NOT DIFFICULT. YOU CAN RECITE IT TO ME INDEPENDENTLY OR, FOR EXTRA CREDIT, IN FRONT OF THE CLASS.

FOR ME, THERE WAS ONLY ONE CHOICE WITH MY MEXICAN PRONUNCIATION: TO RECITE THE PASSAGE TO HER PRIVATELY.
I KNEW I HAD A THICK ACCENT, NOT BECAUSE I HEARD IT MYSELF, BUT BECAUSE KIDS SOMETIMES MADE FUN OF ME WHEN I SPOKE ENGLISH.

ON THE BUS, I TRIED TO MEMORIZE THE SECTION FROM THE DECLARATION OF INDEPENDENCE, BUT I HAD TROUBLE CONCENTRATING.
I KEPT WONDERING WHAT MR. SIMS HAD TOLD ROBERTO.

WHEN I GOT HOME AND SAW THE CARCACHITA, I KNEW ROBERTO WAS ALREADY THERE.

WHAT HAPPENED?
TELL ME!

WHAT DO YOU THINK?!

YOU GOT A JOB!

YES—
MR. SIMS OFFERED ME THE JANITORIAL JOB AT MAIN STREET SCHOOL!
IT'S A YEAR-ROUND JOB.

EDUCATION PAYS OFF, MI'JO. I AM PROUD OF YOU.
TOO BAD YOUR MAMÁ AND I DIDN'T HAVE THE OPPORTUNITY TO GO TO SCHOOL.
BUT YOU'VE TAUGHT US A LOT, PAPÁ.

I WAS SO EXCITED ABOUT ROBERTO'S NEW JOB THAT IT WAS DIFFICULT TO FOCUS ON MY HOMEWORK.
BUT I WAS DETERMINED TO RECITE THE WORDS FROM THE DECLARATION OF INDEPENDENCE PERFECTLY.
I BROKE THE TEXT DOWN, LINE BY LINE.
I LOOKED IN THE DICTIONARY FOR THE WORDS I DID NOT KNOW: *SELF-EVIDENT, ENDOWED, UNALIENABLE, PURSUIT.*
THEN I WROTE THE ENTIRE TEXT IN MY NEW BLACK NOTEPAD.
MY PLAN WAS TO MEMORIZE AT LEAST ONE LINE A DAY.

ON TUESDAY AFTER SCHOOL, ROBERTO DROVE TO EL CAMINO JUNIOR HIGH...

...TO PICK ME UP SO THAT I COULD HELP HIM CLEAN MAIN STREET SCHOOL.

THE FIRST CLASSROOM WE WERE TO CLEAN BROUGHT BACK MEMORIES. IT WAS THE SAME ROOM I HAD USED IN THE FIRST GRADE, WHEN I HAD HAD MISS SCALAPINO. EVERYTHING LOOKED THE SAME EXCEPT THAT THE DESKS AND CHAIRS SEEMED A LOT SMALLER.

I SAT DOWN AT THE TEACHER'S DESK, TOOK OUT MY NOTEPAD, AND WROTE:
"WE HOLD THESE TRUTHS TO BE SELF-EVIDENT,"
"THAT THEY ARE ENDOWED BY THEIR CREATOR WITH CERTAIN UNALIENABLE RIGHTS, THAT AMONG THESE ARE LIFE, LIBERTY AND THE PURSUIT OF HAPPINESS."

"THAT ALL MEN ARE CREATED EQUAL, THAT THEY ARE ENDOWED BY THEIR CREATOR WITH CERTAIN UNALIENABLE RIGHTS,"

"THAT AMONG THESE ARE LIFE, LIBERTY AND THE PURSUIT OF HAPPINESS,"

PUSH
"—THAT TO SECURE THESE RIGHTS, GOVERNMENTS ARE INSTITUTED AMONG MEN, DERIVING THEIR JUST POWERS FROM THE CONSENT OF THE GOVERNED."

WITHIN A FEW DAYS, I HAD MEMORIZED THE LINES. BUT ONE WORD KEPT CAUSING ME PROBLEMS.
UN-
A-
LI-
EN-
A-
BLE...

ARE YOU TRYING TO SAY SOMETHING?
NO... WHY DO YOU ASK?

WELL, YOU KEEP MOVING YOUR LIPS.
WHEN I TOLD HIM WHAT I WAS DOING, I DON'T THINK HE BELIEVED ME.

ON FRIDAY, THE SCHOOL DAY STARTED OUT JUST RIGHT.
IN THE MORNING, MR. MILO ASKED US TO REARRANGE OUR SEATS ACCORDING TO OUR TEST SCORES.

I SAT IN THE FIRST SEAT IN THE FIRST ROW.

AT ONE O'CLOCK, RIGHT AFTER LUNCH, I WAS THE FIRST ONE IN MISS EHLIS'S CLASSROOM. I SAT AT MY DESK AND WENT OVER THE RECITATION IN MY MIND ONE LAST TIME.

"WE HOLD THESE TRUTHS..."

THIS IS HIM...
THE INSTANT I SAW THE GREEN UNIFORM I WANTED TO RUN, BUT MY LEGS WOULD NOT MOVE.
I BEGAN TO TREMBLE AND COULD FEEL MY HEART POUNDING AS THOUGH IT WANTED TO ESCAPE TOO.

MY EYES CLOUDED, AND, FEELING DIZZY AND CONFUSED,
I FOLLOWED THE IMMIGRATION OFFICER INTO HIS CAR.

U.S. GOVERNMENT
388485

...TO PICK UP ROBERTO.

THE END

AUTHOR'S NOTE

The Circuit, like its sequels *Breaking Through, Reaching Out,* and *Taking Hold,* is a memoir. It is based on my childhood experiences of growing up in a family of migrant farm workers. My intent in relating these experiences from the child's point of view is to have readers hear the child's voice, see through his eyes, and feel through his heart.

In writing *The Circuit,* I relied heavily on my childhood recollections, but I also did a lot of background research to help me remember the past. I interviewed my mother, my older brother, Roberto, and other relatives. I looked through old photographs and family documents and listened to corridos—Mexican ballads—that I had heard as a child. I went to different places in the San Joaquin Valley where we had lived in migrant labor camps: Fresno, Orosi, Selma, Corcoran, Five Points. I visited museums in those towns and read through newspapers from that era. I found little or no information or documentation in those sources about migrant farm workers. I was disappointed but more convinced that I should write this book.

I wrote *The Circuit* to record part of my family's history but also, and more important, to give readers an insight into the lives of migrant farmworker families from the past and the present whose hard and noble work of picking fruits and vegetables puts food on our tables. What sustains these families, toiling day after day, are their courage, faith, and hopes and dreams for a better life for their children and their children's children. Their story is an integral part of the American story.

My hope is that readers of my work will deepen their empathy, respect, and appreciation for immigrants, some of whom are migrant farm workers, whose invaluable contributions have shaped who we are as a nation.

FRANCISCO, ROBERTO, AND TRAMPITA IN TENT CITY, SANTA MARIA, CA.

GLOSSARY

ABUELITA: GRANDMA

ABUELITO: GRANDPA

ALLÁ: THERE; OVER THERE

EL ÁNGEL DE ORO: THE GOLDEN ANGEL

¡AY, DIOS MÍO!: OH MY GOD!

LA BOLA: THE HARVEST OF COTTON LEFT OVER FROM THE FIRST PICKING, INCLUDING SHELLS AND LEAVES; SOMETIMES REFERRED TO AS THE SECOND PICKING

BRACERO: FARM LABORER; A MEXICAN LABORER ALLOWED INTO THE UNITED STATES FOR A LIMITED TIME AS A SEASONAL AGRICULTURAL WORKER

CAMPESINO: A PEASANT FARMWORKER OR FARMER

CARCACHITA: OLD JALOPY; AN OLD CAR

CARNE CON CHILE: MEAT WITH CHILI

COMAL: A SMOOTH, FLAT GRIDDLE TYPICALLY USED IN MEXICO TO COOK TORTILLAS

¿CÓMO SE DICE "ES TUYO" EN INGLÉS?: HOW DO YOU SAY "IT'S YOURS" IN ENGLISH?

CONTRATISTA: CONTRACTOR; PERSON WHO HIRES FARM LABORERS

CORRIDO: BALLAD IN A TRADITIONAL MEXICAN STYLE, TYPICALLY HAVING LYRICS THAT NARRATE A HISTORICAL EVENT

CURANDERA: A WOMAN HEALER WHO USES FOLK REMEDIES

DIOS LO QUIERA: GOD WILLING.

ES MUY BUENA GENTE: HE/SHE IS VERY NICE/A VERY GOOD PERSON.

LA FRONTERA: THE BORDER SEPARATING MEXICO FROM CALIFORNIA

FELIZ NAVIDAD: MERRY CHRISTMAS.

FRIJOLES DE LA OLLA: BEANS BOILED IN A POT

GRACIAS A DIOS: THANK GOD.

HACENDADO: OWNER OF A HACIENDA

HACIENDA: A LARGE ESTATE OR PLANTATION

¡HOLA!: HELLO!

HUERQUITO: LITTLE KID

LIBRITO: LITTLE NOTEBOOK; LITTLE BOOK

EL MAL DE OJO: THE EVIL EYE; A FOLK BELIEF IN AN EVIL SPELL PRIMARILY CAST ON CHILDREN

MI'JA: MY DAUGHTER; EXPRESSED WITH AFFECTION, ENDEARMENT

MI'JITO: MY LITTLE SON; EXPRESSED WITH AFFECTION, ENDEARMENT

MI'JO: MY SON; EXPRESSED WITH AFFECTION, ENDEARMENT

LA MIGRA: A SLANG TERM FOR IMMIGRATION LAW ENFORCEMENT AGENTS

MI OLLA: MY POT

MOCOSO: YOUNG KID; SNOTTY KID

¡NO SEAS TONTO!: DON'T BE STUPID/FOOLISH!

¡OTRA VEZ LA BURRA AL TRIGO!: HERE WE GO AGAIN! LITERALLY, "THE DONKEY BACK AGAIN TO THE WHEAT."

PAISANO: FELLOW COUNTRYMAN

PERICO: PARROT

PERIQUITO: LITTLE PARROT; EXPRESSED WITH AFFECTION, ENDEARMENT

¡PERIQUITO BONITO!: BEAUTIFUL LITTLE PARROT!

QUE DIOS LOS BENDIGA: MAY GOD BLESS YOU.

QUINCE: FIFTEEN

SANTA MARÍA, MADRE DE DIOS, RUEGA SEÑORA...: HOLY MARY, MOTHER OF GOD, PRAY FOR US SINNERS NOW AND IN THE HOUR OF OUR DEATH, AMEN.

SANTO NIÑO DE ATOCHA: HOLY INFANT OF ATOCHA; ROMAN CATHOLIC IMAGE OF THE CHRIST CHILD

SE HAN VUELTO LOCOS: THEY'VE GONE CRAZY.

SI: IF

SÍ: YES

SOLEDAD: SOLITUDE OR LONELINESS

TACO: A TORTILLA FOLDED AROUND A FILLING AND EATEN BY HAND

TIENEN QUE TENER CUIDADO: YOU HAVE TO BE CAREFUL.

TONTO: FOOLISH; STUPID

TORTILLA: A TYPE OF THIN FLATBREAD, TYPICALLY MADE OF CORN OR WHEAT FLOUR

VÁMONOS: LET'S GO.

¡VÁMONOS AL HOSPITAL!: LET'S GO TO THE HOSPITAL!

VERDOLAGAS: PURSLANE; A WILD SPINACH-TYPE PLANT

VIEJA: OLD LADY; EXPRESSED WITH AFFECTION, ENDEARMENT

VIEJO: OLD MAN; EXPRESSED WITH AFFECTION, ENDEARMENT

VIRGEN DE GUADALUPE: OUR LADY OF GUADALUPE, PATRONESS OF THE AMERICAS

YA ES HORA: IT'S TIME.

¡YA, PUES!: ENOUGH, ALREADY!

READ MORE BY FRANCISCO JIMÉNEZ

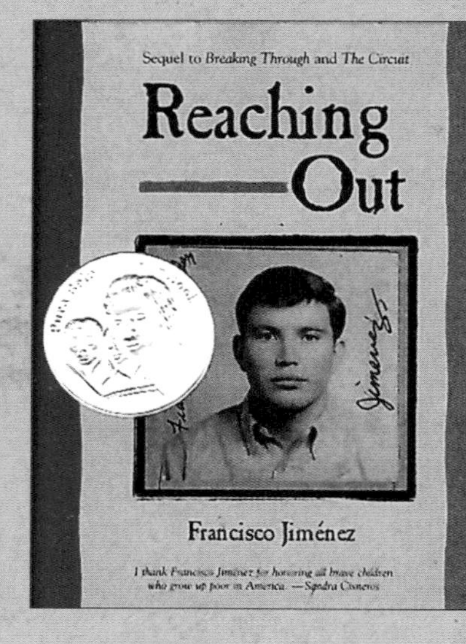

"WRITTEN IN GORGEOUS, ECONOMICAL PROSE, THIS QUARTET'S IMPORTANCE CONTINUES TO GROW."
—BOOKLIST'S 50 BEST YA BOOKS OF ALL TIME

"THE FAMILY'S ODYSSEY IS HEARTRENDING, BUT IT IS THE TRUTH, AND IT'S SKILLFULLY TOLD BY SOMEONE WHO'S BEEN THERE."
—RUDOLFO ANAYA